NEVER
TOO LATE FOR
LOVE

J.E. DUKE

This revised and expanded edition is the first version released in both e-book and print form. Future publications will be available for download and/or in print at most online retailers

Visit the author's website.
www.jeduke.com

As always, to my family.

A special Mahalo to Wilma Dela Cruz

Chapter 1

Happy New Year

For the past three years, Douglas Hedges has had a ritual on the first day of work in January. He stops by the front door and reads the framed email from his ex-wife, as he leaves for the office.

"Douglas, I've filed for divorce!
Elizabeth and I are moving out of state.
Vivian."

Each time he reads the email, he re-lives the moment when he received it. He remembers calling Vivian's cell phone which was disconnected and then when he arrived at their apartment, he found that she had packed up everything in the place except whatever was on his desk. Douglas always blamed the situation on his non-stop work schedule which really didn't allow him much free time to socialize. He hadn't been able to see anyone on a regular basis. *"I guess,"* Douglas thought, *"I'm a confirmed bachelor - - and there's nothing wrong with that!"*

As he locked his West L.A. condo, he took a deep breath of L.A. air and said, "It's going to be a good first work day of the year...I can feel it." Douglas pulled out of his parking space, turned onto the narrow West L.A.

street, and headed toward his office in downtown Los Angeles. "I was right; it is a slow traffic day," he muttered as he arrived at the building. There was a hand-made sign stuck on two saw horses across the driveway at the parking garage.

"Lot closed for re-surfacing
park on the street."

Well, it *was* looking like a great first day. He headed back to the street, waited for the light to change and found an empty parking space on the next block with a broken meter! Douglas stopped, waved the car behind him around, and began to parallel park. He surprised himself. He did it in one move. But just to make sure, he backed up a little bit more and bumped the car behind him. He shook his head and muttered, "I was doing so well, too."

Douglas got out slowly, looking for traffic and moved to the rear of his car. He noticed that he **did** bump the older yellow VW bug parked behind him. It wasn't bad, just a cracked left front headlight. Douglas took a business card from his pocket and left a short note, which he placed under the wiper blades. Then, as an afterthought, he used his cell phone to snap a photo of the damage. Douglas liked the VW bug which seemed in good condition for a 1986 or 1987. It's hard to tell them apart.

As he bent down to retrieve his briefcase, he noticed a black portfolio (approx. 36" x 36") on the ground halfway under the rear of his car. He picked it up, looked around, and not seeing anyone, decided to take it with him to the office. Johnny, the building security guard, opened the door for him, "I haven't seen you in a while Mr. Hedges, Happy New Year." Douglas didn't have a free-hand but managed a smile and a return greeting as he waited for the elevator. His cell phone rang and he fumbled with it for a moment. "Yes, Marge, I'm almost there, just seven floors away, be right up." The elevator ride to the Lawson Law Group on the seventh floor was smooth and quiet! Then the doors opened and Marge met Douglas with a New Year's greeting and a stack of files. "We've got a semi-busy day. So, let's get crackin'." *"I really do want to know who works for whom"*, Douglas thought, as he entered his corner office, looked out at the vista and beyond and called out "HAPPY NEW YEAR L.A."

Marge was standing and waiting for instructions as Douglas turned to her. Even at five-foot-one, Douglas knew that his sergeant-like assistant was all-business. She's the one that kept him organized and had helped him stay at the top of his game for the past twelve years. In her mind, she always thought, *"Every lawyer needs a Marge."* Douglas asked her to call Scott Brewer. She scrunched her face a bit as she looked at him, "That's your auto insurance agent. What did you do now?" Douglas looked at her sheepishly, "Well, I had a slight fender bender this morning. Before you ask me, yes, I left a note, so Scott will probably get a call soon". Marge returned to her desk and said, "Will do. And you have a meeting with B & B Fashions."

Douglas opened his briefcase and removed a wrapped package with a "Happy New Year" bow. He messed with the bow and then centered the package on the desk. Marge buzzed to say that his insurance agent was in a meeting and would get back to him ASAP! "Thank you, Marge. What time is my B & B meeting and where?" About five seconds later she walked in with a coffee service on a tray leading Bernie & Bernice of B & B Fashions and announced, "The meeting is here...and now!" Douglas exchanged New Year's greetings and friendly hugs with Bernie & Bernice and said, "Please sit and tell me what's up. This is my first meeting of the first work day of the year."

Douglas has been B & B's attorney for a long time, even before he joined The Lawson Law Group. He'd helped them with their trademarks, various contracts and made a few court appearances on their behalf. He really likes the older couple. They are very honest and extremely reliable. If they say they will do something or will be somewhere at a certain time, they always keep their word. Bernie explained that B & B fashions wanted to start a new division. Until now, they had concentrated on a mid-price line of all-around fashions for women.

The company made products for many design houses under various labels and were in many big-box stores across the country. Now they wanted to start marketing resort wear and other fashions under their own brand name. They explained to Douglas that they needed his help to set up the new company and trademarks. They were planning to start to interview some new designers today and wanted to get this project moving as soon as possible.

Bernie wanted to know what Douglas thought of their new idea. He smiled, "I see people wearing resort stuff everywhere, so there must be a market for it."

Bernice commented, "We have appointments with several swim suit designers today." Bernie smiled as he placed several files on Douglas' desk. "These are our notes about our new idea. Look them over and let us know if you need more info." B & B left the office smiling.

Marge stepped in and said, "Your insurance agent is on line one." As Douglas picked up the phone, he handed her the small gift box and said, "Here, this has your name on it. Hi Scott, thank you for calling and Happy New Year to you too. Scott, I backed into a parked car today and damaged the left-front headlight. I left my card and your phone number so I'm sure you'll be hearing from the owner. I'll fax you the license plate number and the location. Okay, gotta run." Douglas began to read B & B's stack of notes as Marge and her gift headed to her desk. The morning flashed by and before he knew it, lunch time came and went and the day was almost over. It was NOT a semi-busy day, as promised. There were many New Year's phone calls and interruptions.

Marge walked into the office modeling her "gift". "Thank you so much for this pretty scarf." Douglas looked up and said, "You're very welcome, just something to say Happy New Year! Where is everybody today?" Marge shrugged her shoulders, "I guess they're taking an extra holiday. The first day of the year is almost over for us." She noticed the black portfolio and commented, "Is this from a new client?"

Douglas told her that he'd forgotten all about the portfolio. "I found it under my car when I parked this morning. I had to park on the street since they were re-surfacing our lot." Marge gave him a sly smile as she said, "I parked in our lot. Oh, but then I was here early!"

Douglas opened the portfolio to find fashion designs and photos. He and Marge looked at all of the drawings which were very professionally drawn and displayed a wide range of styles. He looked at Marge and said, "I bet the person who lost this must be frantic."

She agreed and held up a dress design, "It took a long time to create these. I really like this one. Oh, here's a business card." Douglas called the number on the Devin Designs card. "Hi, is this Devin Clark?" A young woman replied, "No, she's not here right now. She'll be back later today." Douglas continued, "I'm calling about a black portfolio that I found in the street this morning. I think it's hers. May I come over and drop it off?" The young woman told him she would be there for a while.

He picked up the portfolio and started out the door but remembered he needed to fax some information to the insurance company. He gave Marge a sheet of paper with the license number of the car and the accident location. "Marge, please fax this information to the insurance company to the attention of Scott. I'm going to drop this portfolio off in Silver Lake on my way home. Call me on my cell if you need me." Just as the elevator door was closing he heard Marge call out, "Thanks again for the scarf."

Down in the street, Douglas noticed a tow truck next to his car. They were hooking up the yellow VW bug parked behind him and were ready to tow it. Pointing to the VW, the tow driver asked, "Is this your car?" Douglas replied, "No this one is mine." The driver told him, "Well you just made it! We're impounding all these cars. Didn't you see the sign? I'll pull my truck back a little so it will be easier for you to get out." Douglas and the driver exchanged New Year's greetings and as Douglas drove off, he finally saw the sign.

TUESDAY - January 3
NO PARKING AFTER 4 PM
All Cars will be towed
L.A. Impound Lot #264

He thought that the New Year was starting off okay for him and those two tow truck drivers, but not for the owners of all those other cars! He muttered, "Guess they didn't see the sign either. Next stop, Silver Lake." Douglas set his GPS to the address on the business card and the automated voice did her thing. He arrived at Devin Clark's Silver Lake apartment in about 20 minutes. He grabbed the portfolio and headed for the front door. Looking over the list of tenants, there was a "D. Clark 314," he pushed the announce button.

Over the scratchy loud speaker, he heard, *"You the guy who called?"* Douglas answered and moments later, he heard the familiar buzzer. He entered the trendy apartment house and knocked at #314. A lady's voice called out, "It's open, come on in."

When Douglas entered the neatly arranged apartment, he saw a drafting table against one wall with an array of clothing designs, material swatches and photos. The table and the kitchen were the only areas that weren't "neat-as-a-pin." Douglas saw an attractive

7

young woman pouring beer into tall glasses on the kitchen island. He said, "Hello, I called earlier about finding this portfolio." The young woman replied, "Yes, that's Devin's. She's a designer. I'm Shelly. Happy New Year, you want a beer?"

Shelly finished pouring as Douglas counted nine full glasses on the counter. "No thanks, not right now. Are you having a party?" Shelly grinned, "No, I'm an actress and I have a beer commercial tomorrow. I have to do a "PERFECT POUR" on command."

There was a knock at the door and Shelly yelled, "It's open, Happy New Year!" David, a next-door neighbor entered and asked if Shelly was still pouring beer? She held up a full glass and he asked, "Are you still doing cat food for the other audition?" She said she finished that but hadn't dumped the food. "Okay then, I'll take some food for the outside cats and a few beers for the inside cats,"

Shelly handed David a tray filled with beer and open cans of cat food. "This is David. David, this is um…" Douglas quickly replied, "I'm Douglas Hedges. I found this portfolio and just wanted to return it. Tell Ms. Clark to call me if she needs any information. Here's my card and it was nice meeting you."

David looked at the tray and said, "Nice pour job, huh?" Douglas quickly replied, "Yes, I guess it is. I'm not a good judge of pouring beer, but they do look good. You'll make sure she gets the portfolio?" Shelly escorted the guys to the door and said, "Yes, I'll make sure she gets it and Happy New Year to both of you."

Douglas' phone rang as he was leaving the condo. "Yes Marge, what's up?" Marge said, "I just wanted to thank you again for the scarf and tell you there's a staff meeting at nine-thirty tomorrow morning." As Douglas headed back to West L.A., he thought, *It looks like it's going to be a nice evening and maybe this year is off to a good start.* The next morning, Douglas found normal, heavy L.A. traffic, which meant a call to Marge to say he might be a few minutes late. She told him to park in the building because the lot was finished. "But, hurry!" Marge was waiting in the hallway as Douglas stepped off the elevator. She didn't say a word, she just pointed toward the conference room. Douglas muttered, "How does she know when I arrive. Spies! That's it the building is full of spies."

Douglas entered the conference room and joined the meeting which had just started. Mr. Michael Lawson, head of The Lawson Law Group, and several attorneys were seated at the conference table. Mr. Lawson spotted him and said, "Douglas has been working already this week. What do you have for us?" Douglas looked around the room, "Good morning and Happy New Year everybody. Yesterday I had an early meeting with B & B Fashions. They want us to handle the expansion of their business."

Mr. Lawson acknowledged his announcement and said, "I'm glad to see that the New Year is off to a great start. I've seen the tally of hours billed last year. At the top of the list we find Mr. Christopher in third place, Miss Shilling is in second place and the top lawyer in billable hours is Douglas Hedges!" Everyone in the room gave them a round of polite applause.

Mr. Lawson continued, "Everyone will be receiving their yearly bonuses at the company conference in March. Thank you for your diligent work and let's hope that this year is even bigger." The room cleared fast as everybody headed back to their offices.

Douglas walked down the hall and as he passed Marge, he motioned for her to come with him. As they entered his office he said, "Okay, before you try to pry things out of me…" Marge cut him off, smiled and said, "I know, you were the top guy last year and Mr. Lawson said you're getting an award." Douglas looked at her with a puzzled frown and said, "Yes, that's what I was going to say, but how do you know that?" Marge just grinned.

Back in his office Douglas began to look over the papers left for him by B & B Fashions. He told Marge all about the black portfolio and his trip to Silver Lake. They both had a good laugh about the cat food & beer!

Chapter 2

A Lawyer Should Know Better

The year was off to a very busy start. Douglas was handling two corporate mergers, an arbitration hearing and several contract disputes. He was also spending a lot of time working on the new B & B expansion. Since B & B had been with him so long, he tended to give them a little extra time, for which they never seemed to get billed. But all this work won't matter, if B & B couldn't find suitable designers. They were still looking. Douglas glanced at his desk calendar, "It's already Friday, January thirteenth, where does the time go?"

Marge buzzed him, "Your auto insurance guy is on line one." Douglas moved a few papers and uncovered his phone. "Hi Scott! You heard from the owner of the car I bumped?"

"Yes, I did." The insurance agent told him he was at the impound lot, he'd talked with the car's owner and he found the note Douglas left at the scene. Douglas felt a bit relieved, "So, you'll take care of everything then?" Scott answered, *"Well, yes and no. Can you come over to the impound lot?"* Douglas covered the mouthpiece while he asked Marge what he was doing the rest of the day. She looked at his schedule and told him he was booked till two-thirty and then had a meeting at five-thirty at the

Italian Grotto Restaurant in Malibu. He scribbled the address of the impound lot and told Scott he'd be there in about an hour.

Douglas asked Marge to pull the papers for The Grotto and told her he was going to meet Scott in about hour. When the scheduled day was over, Marge handed him the papers for the Malibu restaurant which he put in his briefcase. "Marge, I will be on my cell phone and I probably won't be back today. You know when you go to the Grotto, Tony feeds you." Marge had always wanted to visit this spectacular restaurant but never could. "Next time, you go with me."

Douglas exited the elevator at the parking level and hopped in his car. He didn't really know where he was going. He checked his notes and entered the location into his GPS. "Thank goodness for these devices." He muttered as he pulled into Impound Lot #264 and after a few minutes, he found visitor parking which wasn't easy to locate because the lot had cars parked everywhere. After a short, dusty walk, he finally found Scott waiting for him at the towing office. "Douglas, thanks for coming. I called the owner and she should be here soon. Let's take a look at the car you hit." Douglas looked at Scott and defiantly said, "HIT? No, I just bumped a car when I was parking. I DID NOT hit anything!"

They began to walk down a very long row of cars. Some were covered in thick soot, and a few had seen better days. They even saw a couple of new-shiny models and then they came to an abrupt stop. Scott removed a piece of paper from his jacket pocket. "I've got your note here. It's written on the back of your business card which is attached to the impound sheet. Let's see what it says." He looked at Douglas as he read, "I damaged your car while parking. Call my insurance agent Scott Brewer at Trident Insurance, he'll arrange for repair. Signed, D. Hedges. Is that what you wrote?" Douglas thought for a moment, took the card and answered, "Yes, that's what I wrote." Scott took him by the arm, and led him toward the VW. "OK, let's take a look at the car you bumped. I'm glad you sent over the license plate number and accident location. That made it easy to find the owner. Here's the car #207-22. I would say it's more than just a bump."

The yellow VW bug looked as if it had been in a demolition derby. The paint was scraped all over. The driver's door & window were smashed in. The hood was mangled, so was the rear panel. The roof had a very large dent as if something had fallen on it. The door handles and the radio antenna were lying on the dashboard. Douglas walked around the car shaking his head. "I didn't do all this!" He stopped and pointed at the left front headlight. "I did that." He gestured toward the car. "Scott, I didn't do all this! How did this happen?" Scott smiled as he approached the barrister. "Well, according to your note, you did it. You wrote, and I quote, I damaged your car." Douglas was at a loss for words, as a taxi pulled into the lot. Scott looked up and saw a female passenger. "That might be the owner."

Douglas and Scott looked on as a very attractive young lady was being directed toward them. They watched as Devin Clark, sporting a cast on her right arm, approached. She was a strikingly beautiful woman with a model's stride. Her long brown hair flowed in the breeze as she crossed the lot. Scott said quietly, "That's a great-looking lady!" He and Douglas approached the young woman. "Ms. Clark? I'm Scott Brewer and this is my client Douglas Hedges." Devin looked beyond the men and starred at the mangled VW. "Is this my car? Is it really my car?" She reached in through the broken window and found one of her business cards wedged between the seats. "It is my car. How did all this happen?"

Douglas didn't know what to say so Scott added, "Well, Mr. Hedges says he just bumped your car as he was parking. He says he only damaged the left front headlight." Scott was waiting for Douglas to continue. It took a moment, but he finally did. "Your car was parked on the street in downtown and that's where I bumped it. It was towed here, because you were in a no-parking zone. So, the damage might have happened when it was towed. What is your name again?"

The young lady said, "Devin Clark." Douglas wondered why her name was so familiar. She smiled and said, "You returned my portfolio." He suddenly remembered, "Yes, the portfolio. Sorry I forgot. That was a couple of weeks ago." Devin raised her cast, "Seems longer for me, I have a broken arm and now a broken car. But I'm sure thankful that you returned my portfolio Mr. Hedges." The young designer moved around to the other side of the VW and Scott turned to Douglas. "I have to tell you that it looks like we might have to repair the entire automobile. If so, that's going to cost you a lot. If we only had a witness or a photo of the original damage, we could sue the impound lot. Do you have a photo or was there a witness?"

"I think I have a photo." Douglas attempted to open his media file, but the phone was slow to respond. He tried again and got an error message. **FILE CORRUPTED**. "I do have a photo, but I can't retrieve it. The file's corrupted." He showed the screen to Scott. "So, I guess I don't have a photo and there were no witnesses, except for the tow truck drivers."

Scott shrugged his shoulders and turned to Devin. "Ms. Clark, our company will have your car moved to a repair facility and have it fully restored. I'll contact you when I know the completion date." Devin began to smile for the first time since arriving at the lot. "Really! You'll fix it back to the way it was? But Mr. Hedges said he only broke the headlight." Scott told her that may be true, but without a photo, we have to rely on the note Mr. Hedges left at the scene. He handed the business card to Devin. She read the note for the first time. Scott told her, "We'll restore your VW. It will be as good as new." Devin couldn't believe it. "Thank you, Mr. Brewer and Mr. Hedges. Now, I just have to get this cast off so I can get back to work drawing and designing and hopefully finding a job."

Scott excused himself and headed toward the impound lot's office. He turned back toward Douglas and held up the note. "A Lawyer should know better. We'll talk soon." Devin called out, "Thank you again." She asked Douglas if she could use his phone to call a cab. Douglas smiled, "No need for that, I can drop you at your apartment. Remember, I was there once so it's programmed into my GPS." Devin thanked him again as they crossed the lot attempting not to step in any oil or debris.

During the short trip, Devin was excited that her car would be fixed. She thanked Douglas again for returning her portfolio. They had a good laugh when he told her about meeting Shelly and the cat food and beer incident. "Does she do that often?" Devin shook her head, "No, not often, only when she has an audition." Douglas laughed, "It must be hard with a roommate like that." "She's not my roommate. Shelly lives down the hall, and doesn't like to mess up her place."

Devin quickly explained her accident too. She was on her way to a meeting in downtown to show her designs. She left the portfolio on the top of her car when she locked it. When she got into the crosswalk she realized she didn't have it. "I turned to go back to the car and didn't look both ways. That's when I got hit in the crosswalk, someone called 911 and I ended up in the hospital. I never thought I'd ever see my portfolio again." She thanked Douglas, many times! Before they knew it, they had talked all the way to her apartment. As Devin closed the car door she thanked him again. Douglas told her to keep him posted on the car.

He watched as Devin started toward her apartment. He thought she looked terrific. *"I wonder if she's attached?"* He made a quick call to Marge to ask her to contact The Grotto. "I can't get there today. It's too late and the traffic will be miserable. I'll see you in the morning." Devin picked up her mail and waved to him as she headed up the stairs. Douglas smiled as he thought, *"I may have to revise my thinking; this year is looking good!"*

Chapter 3

A Perfect Pour

It was a few minutes past nine AM when Douglas stepped off the elevator. Marge was waiting in the hallway with several messages. The first thing she wanted to know was how the fender-bender worked out yesterday. "It's all taken care of. I need to get a lot done on the B & B expansion today. Would you bring in their file?" As Marge went to her desk to retrieve the file, Douglas set up a white board in his office and began to map out a strategy for B & B. He wrote **WEBSITE?? - Sub directory: Resort Fashions - Major Lines - Men - Women - Shoes? Social Media accounts.** Marge entered and placed the file on his desk. She looked at his white board scribbles. She asked, "Do they have a website?" Douglas didn't know for sure, "Better get Bernie on the phone, I'll ask." Douglas continued to write on the white board... **Photos - Drawings - Models - email - logo - TM ®, DESIGNERS?? Swimwear, Men & Women??**

Marge told him that Bernie was on line one. Douglas began to ask about everything he had written on the white board. He made notes as they talked. "Oh okay, we need to take care of all that stuff. We'll talk soon." Douglas had one final question. "Did you find any designers, yet?" They hadn't found anybody for sure. "Are you only looking for people with experience?" Bernie said, "I don't care as long as they have ideas and can draw." Douglas told him that he might have an idea for them. "Let's talk later." Marge asked, "So, what's their website?" Douglas circled that on the whiteboard. "They don't have one, nor any social networking or even email. B & B is very old-school. Now it's time to become very NEW SCHOOL! I'll give you some notes on this later today or tomorrow. Better get in touch with our consulting firm. I think we'll need them on this project."

Marge started to leave the office, "When you're finished, give me your notes and I'll add them to the file." Douglas circled DESIGNERS in red. "Marge, I was thinking about something last night." She stopped to listen. "Yesterday, at the impound lot I met the owner of the car I bumped. You remember the portfolio with the fashion drawings?" Marge was suddenly intrigued. "Yes, I remember the drawings, why?" Douglas added another circle around DESIGNERS on his board. "Those designs were hers. The car I bumped belongs to the person who designed all those fashions. Now, I really believe in the "small world" concept. Anyway, she's never worked in that industry, but she'd like to."

Marge needed more information. "So, what were you thinking?" Douglas pointed to the white board, "I was thinking that maybe she should talk to Bernice. Perhaps B & B could give her some advice." Marge agreed and then had a thought. "Ah, wait a minute, a girl?

Is she pretty, is she tall? Is she married? Douglas moved to his desk chair. "Oh, don't start that again, I don't know!" Marge approached his desk. "Douglas Hedges, in the twelve years I've worked with you, how many girls have you been interested in?" Douglas stared her down, "I'm not interested in her. I just want to help. The answer to your question is, not too many." Marge smiled and said, "Not interested. Okay, I'll buy that. You just want to help. I'm going to make a note that you said that." Marge put his quote in her book as she turned to leave. Douglas stopped her by saying, "I just felt a little sorry for her. She has a broken arm and her car is a mess. It won't be running for several weeks." Marge softened her attack. "Okay, then. Maybe I do buy it. A little advice from Bernie and Bernice might be helpful."

The day passed quickly as Douglas concentrated on his phone calls, keeping the call log, which he usually forgot. He also worked on B & B's expansion. The sun was going down when Marge popped her head in the door. "How late are you staying? Do you need me?" Douglas looked up and told her he was fine, "I'll see you tomorrow."

Marge and several of her co-workers packed up and headed to the elevator. Douglas wrapped up his current business and started stacking files neatly on the edge of his desk. He opened his briefcase and began to add a few items. He looked around to make sure he hadn't forgotten anything and noticed that his cell phone was flashing. He had missed a call from Scott, his insurance agent. Douglas put the phone on speaker while he finished packing his briefcase.

"Doug, this is Scott…we've assessed the damage to the VW and it works out this way. We'll pay for most of the claim. Your portion will be about twelve-hundred dollars, unless you want to contest it. If not, let me know and we'll get started on the repairs.

Call me tomorrow!"

Douglas thought for a moment and left a message for Scott. *"Hi, Scott, this is Doug Hedges. Go ahead with the repairs, and you're right, I should have known better."* As he drove to his condo, Douglas placed a call to Bernie and Bernice. They laughed when he told them they weren't on the clock. "I wondered if you found any designers?" Bernie said there were two that they liked, "But we're still looking." Douglas told them that he met a designer yesterday. Bernie asked how and where they met and Douglas explained all about the accident, the portfolio and the drawings. "What I saw looked pretty good." Douglas admitted that he didn't know much about the fashion business or this young lady. He just wondered if they could meet with Devin, look at her work, and give her some advice. The drive to West L.A. always seemed shorter when he was on the phone. He kept talking to Bernie as he unlocked his front door.

B & B told Douglas to have Devin call them. They would be at the Fashion Mart offices all weekend. "We'll be glad to offer any advice we can. Douglas, I'm glad we weren't on the clock for this conversation. It would have cost us a fortune." They both laughed as Douglas removed a bottle of beer from his under-counter refrigerator. He grabbed an opener and a chilled glass. Douglas joked with Bernie that since they had been clients for over 10 years, their hourly rate was grandfathered-in at the Lawson Legal Group. They were paying about half of what others paid and B & B got a lot of perks too.

Douglas took a few sips of beer while he called Devin. "Hi, Mr. Hedges, I'm glad you called. I want to thank you for helping me yesterday." Douglas told her that he was glad her car would be repaired soon. "Devin, I have an idea for you."

He asked if she'd heard of B & B fashions. She hadn't. He quickly explained his relationship with them and wondered if she would like to meet with Bernie & Bernice. "They know the fashion business and might be able to offer you some advice." Douglas gave her their phone number as he took a second beer from the refrigerator. "Call them tomorrow. They'll be expecting your call." Devin reminded him that when she got her cast off in about two weeks, she wanted to take him to lunch to thank him. Douglas ended the phone call and poured himself another glass of beer; he smiled and said, "I would say this is a perfect pour! Maybe I should do beer commercials."

Chapter 4

Did You Send Flowers?

Douglas checked his desk calendar. "It's February 1ˢᵗ! I can't believe it!" The days were flying by because he'd been up to his hips in work. He had been in arbitration sessions twice last week and two very long meetings with the consulting firm about the B & B expansion. "Marge, can you call B & B and ask when they can meet with us?" She wanted to know what kind of meeting. "Lunch, Dinner?" He said, "Just have them come here to the office. I want to run over all these lists with them and have them meet with Alpha Consulting."

Marge said she'd call them right now. "Did you return all your calls? You had a call from a Devin Clark." Douglas asked when Ms. Clark called. Marge moved to his desk and pulled his call sheet from under a stack of papers. She looked and said, "She called late, yesterday." She handed him the list, "Here! Is that the designer?" Douglas nodded yes and said, "Let me know about B & B"

As soon as he was alone, he called Devin. She was excited to hear from him and said that she met with B & B Fashions and they loved her designs. Douglas thought that was terrific. Devin told him, "They just offered me an internship! I went for some advice and I got a sort-of audition. They like what I've done so far, and want to see what I can do when my cast is off. They said, if I work out, I might have a full-time job there. I'm really excited!"

Douglas was very happy for her. "So, if I get a job, I'll owe you a thank you dinner instead of a thank you lunch. I still can't believe it." Douglas told her that he liked the designs he saw in her portfolio, "Let's see what happens? Call me with updates on your progress at B & B." Devin said they would talk soon. He ended the call and couldn't help smiling. Marge told him that B & B couldn't come to the office for two weeks since they'll be out of town.

He asked her to keep in contact with B & B and set up a meeting date, then let Alpha Consulting know as well. He handed her notes for the meeting. Marge shook her head and said, "There you go smiling again. What is it?" He sluffed it off by saying, "Just good news, that's all." Marge told him, "Well, it's nice to start off the month with good news. Here are a few calls that I took off the service." He looked at the list and put it on the desk. "I'll call them back later."

The day was over before he knew it. This year was beginning to feel like last year, the days were blending together. Marge looked in on Douglas, "Are you feeling okay? You seem to be a bit distracted." He smiled and told her, "I'm fine. I'm just thinking." "Okay thinker, think on this. Mr. Lawson wants you to take a meeting with this client." She handed him a file. "There's a note for you." Douglas took the file and read Mr. Lawson's note.

"Douglas: Please meet with Walter Dennison as soon as possible. He's a long-time client who's been out of the country for a while. He needs a bit of corporate restructuring and some creative thinking. His company is planning a big merger. I think I'll need help on this one."

"Marge, when did Mr. Lawson send this over?" She told him "Just now. Should I call him?" Douglas told Marge that Mr. Lawson wanted him to look over the file first. Douglas continued reading everything as the day began to slip away. Marge entered to find him staring out the window again. "Are you sure you're okay?"

Douglas turned his chair from the window and muttered, "I'm fine. I just have a bunch of stuff on my mind!" She said good night as Douglas continued to read and make notes for Mr. Lawson's client. The work load was taking its toll on Douglas. Each morning he felt as if he hadn't been to bed. As Friday rolled around, he was beginning to wonder what had happened to Wednesday. *"Don't weeks have a Wednesday anymore?"* His days were starting early and ending later and later. But then, with nobody at home, it was better to work late and drop by to see everyone at The Village Tavern several nights a week.

Douglas noticed that there were small flower vases on every desk around the office complex. Experiencing his normal Friday tiredness, Douglas asked, "What's with the flowers?"

Marge pointed to her calendar. "Monday is Valentine's Day. We're just getting in the mood early.

Did you send your mom flowers?" Douglas told her that he had forgotten. She laughed and said, "I knew you'd forget, so I did it for you. I sent myself a bouquet too!" Douglas laughed as he wished her a Happy Valentine's Day. "Did Tony send over the papers for the Grotto?"

Marge suddenly was all business. "No, but you had a call from him a couple days ago. It was in the notes I gave you." Douglas looked on his semi-messy desk and found the list. Douglas placed a call and put it on speaker. "May I speak with Tony, please?" He swung his chair around to look at his wonderful city view. "Hello, is this my favorite chef in the whole wide world? This is Douglas Hedges. You called? Did you have a question about the contracts?" He told Douglas that he couldn't fax the papers because their machine wasn't working. "Should I mail them or would you like to pick them up?"

Marge entered his office. Douglas asked her if he would have time to pick up the papers today. She told him that he could go there a little later. Tony heard her in the background, "Is that Marge?" She smiled and said, "Yes, it's Marge." Tony wondered when he was going to meet her. She told him that Douglas always said he would bring her, but so far it hadn't happened. Douglas told Tony that he would drop by around five-thirty. He promised Marge that he would take her next time. "That's okay. I can't go today. I have to get home and fix dinner for Ralph and then I'm off to my sister's baby shower. Next time for sure!"

Douglas waited until the coast was clear and he called Devin. She was feeling great because she just had her cast removed. Douglas was a little nervous when he said, "That's good. It must be nice not to have that on any more. I wondered if you would like to take a ride out to a restaurant in Malibu this afternoon. I have to pick up some papers and we can celebrate your new arm." Devin had no plans and thought that was a wonderful idea. "Great, I'll pick you up in a few minutes." Douglas put some files in his briefcase and prepared to head out. "I'll see you in the morning. Have fun at the baby shower."

Douglas grabbed his coat, briefcase and cell phone and headed to the elevator. He stopped off on the third floor, hopped in his car and set the GPS. He knew the way, but he just liked to hear the GPS lady talk to him. He kept waiting for her to make a mistake one day. He picked up Devin at her Silver Lake apartment and they headed for the coast. "Off we go. We're going to The Italian Grotto in Malibu! It's the perfect location with the best sunsets in town."

As they drove, Devin now "cast free," showed him the exercises she was supposed to do. She said she felt fine and was back drawing again. She told him about her ideas for B & B. Since she was feeling better she would be able to show them what she could do. During the drive, Douglas talked about his long relationship with B & B.

The restaurant was located on a bluff overlooking the Pacific Ocean. The drive on the coast highway was nice, but he knew the view from the restaurant was fantastic. It was almost sunset when they arrived. The valet opened Devin's door and welcomed them to The Italian Grotto. Douglas took her arm. "I hope you like

Italian!" She smiled, "It's my favorite." Tony saw Douglas and his guest and met them at the door. "Welcome, is this Marge?" Douglas smiled, "No, this is Devin Clark." He looked at Devin and explained that Marge was his secretary.

Tony welcomed them. "Pardon my mistake. Douglas has been here many times but has never brought a guest. One of these times, you better bring Marge! Let me show you to your table." They traversed the restaurant where almost every seat had a fantastic view of the ocean.

Douglas said, "You have some papers for me?" Tony raised his hands to stop Douglas. "First you eat and then we'll talk! It's going to be a wonderful sunset tonight. You're just in time." Douglas and Devin sat and began to soak up the beauty of their surroundings.

Devin thanked him for inviting her to this lovely restaurant. "I never knew this was here." Douglas explained that Tony had been his client and friend for many years. "I love this place and the food is first-rate. I'm glad you met with B & B; they are very nice people. How long have you been drawing?" Devin didn't know for sure. "I've been sketching shoes, hats, dresses, everything since I was a kid." Douglas asked, "If you get the job what do you hope will happen?" She didn't have to think about that question, she was ready with an answer. "I would like them to have some of my pieces produced. Then down the road, I really want to have my own clothing line."

Tony brought over a bottle of imported water and poured each of them a glass. "I know Douglas doesn't drink when he's driving." They both thanked him and

Douglas raised his glass, "Here's to your audition, your new car and your new arm!" Tony placed their salads on the table, "Dinner will be along in a while, relax and enjoy the sunset,"

There is a tradition at The Italian Grotto just as the sun is setting. The entire staff lines up in the rear of the establishment. They watch silently as the sun inches its way to the sea. The restaurant is always quiet at this time. Nobody makes a sound until they see the flash of green light the instant the sun disappears beyond the horizon. When that happens, the staff and most of the long-time patrons burst into applause, and the laughter and the clink of glasses once again takes center stage.

Devin joined in the applause and said, "That was really wonderful!" They began to enjoy their salads. She loved the dressing and asked, "Do they sell it?" Douglas smiled and told his guest that he'd make sure she got a bottle. He was very happy that this lovely lady came into his life. "This is your congratulations dinner." She looked a little confused. "For the car, your arm and your possible job." She stopped eating and smiled.

"Douglas, it's hard for me to believe that I'm finally getting a break. I've been trying for such a long time and nobody would give me a chance. They all want someone with lots of experience. How can you get experience if nobody will hire you? I was about to stop trying and move back with Mom and Dad in Connecticut."

Douglas understood because he faced the same problems when he graduated law school. "Well, I'm glad B & B are letting you try!" Tony approached them with a waiter who put two plates on the table. "Dinner is served. It's eggplant with a small side of spaghetti. Enjoy!"

Douglas smiled and told Devin that he was never given a menu. "Tony always serves me his favorite of the day." She took a whiff and said, "It looks and smells wonderful. They started eating their delightful dinners. It was the best Devin had ever tasted. She was smiling and enjoying her evening away from the drawing table. Douglas wanted to know more about his lovely table mate. "Tell me a little about your design career. Did you study fashion in college?"

Devin gave him a quick peek into her life. "Well, sort-of; I had some art classes and then I changed schools and the new school didn't have many classes, so I took some theatre courses and worked in the costume department. I learned to sew, repair and even got to design some costumes." Douglas thought that was good training. "Do you have to get home at a certain hour?" She didn't. "What about you?"

Douglas told her that nobody was waiting for him. I was married for two years, but not anymore. One day she picked up her daughter from school and left the state. She sent an email saying they were leaving. I know they're alive and well in Southern Texas somewhere, but I don't know where. Devin was shocked by the story. "She sent you an email that she was leaving? That's cold!" Douglas filled her water glass. "Yes, she did. I framed it and hung it in my living room."

Devin wanted to know about his daughter. "Elizabeth was seven at the time, but she isn't mine. She came with the package. I was going to adopt her, but that never happened. That was a little over three years ago! Elizabeth is ten now." Dinner, accompanied by a beautiful sunset on the ocean, was the perfect way to end the week. Douglas and Devin sat in the glow of candles, talking, drinking coffee and sharing a super-scrumptious dessert. To the casual observer, these two people were long-time friends. Nobody would suspect that they had only met a few weeks ago.

Tony was going from table to table with flowers. He stopped in front of Devin. "This rose is for you Signorina. Happy Valentine's Day." Devin was very touched by the gesture and reached up to hug Tony. "Thank you." He smiled at Douglas. "Thank you for bringing this beautiful young lady to my restaurant." Devin was smiling as she held her flower. "You want to know a little more about me?" Douglas stirred his coffee and told her to give him the story. "Well, I've never been married. I got close once, but it didn't happen. I've got a birthday coming up next month. I'm gonna be twenty-nine. Time flies, doesn't it?" Douglas suddenly realized that there was an eleven-year age difference between them. "I've got one on April fifteenth." She smiled and added, "You're a tax baby."

"Yes, that's what they used to call me." Douglas smiled back and then asked, "How did this become such a depressing conversation? I don't like birthdays, never did." Devin said she was sorry, "I just want to get to know you a bit better, that's all." The waiter re-filled their coffee cups. Douglas looked across the table. "All right the fast version. I'm a lawyer who works round-the-clock which is probably why my wife left. But there's good news!" Devin looked at him for the good news.

"About six months ago, I received another email from her, she got re-married! I'm not paying her alimony any more. I printed out that email and gave it to my lawyer. He said you're free! Go have fun, but I'm too busy to have fun or meet people." Devin agreed, "I've been busy trying to get a design job."

Douglas looked across the table and said, "We have the same story except I'm not trying to get a design job. But I have to say it's hard to believe that you're unattached." She wanted to know why he found that hard to believe. Douglas looked for the right words. "Because you're a very beautiful and talented lady." She blushed a bit. "Well, thank you, but since I'm five-feet-ten, most guys don't bother to look my way. They also don't care about my talent. They're only interested in, well, you know!" He understood and told her that he was sorry to hear that. "But for a fashion designer, tall is perfect. I'm six-three and that works for me because I get to stare down at the jury." Devin laughed a little too loud and stopped quickly. "Okay, I guess being tall does have some perks. This is weird, huh?"

He wondered what she meant. She smiled and told him it was like they were on an internet date, but different. He asked if she had ever done that. She shook her head no. "Neither have I. I guess this is similar, but the computer would have never matched us." She looked puzzled. "Why do you say that? I'm tall, you're tall." Douglas leaned in toward her. "I'm also eleven years older than you." She whispered, "You think that matters?" He told her that he thought it did. She shook off the comment by saying, "I'm not sure about that. I think it depends on the person."

Tony interrupted their conversation by placing a manila envelope on the table. "Here are the papers you needed. All signed and ready to go." Douglas thanked him for signing everything, and for dinner." The proud owner said, "No, thank **you** for coming. I hope you'll return!" Devin told him that she loved everything including dessert and her rose. Tony suggested they take a walk on the beach and burn off a few calories. "It's not that chilly." Devin thought that sounded like fun. They said their goodbyes to Tony and walked toward the side stairway which led down to the beach below. It was a semi-chilly California night.

Devin grabbed on to Douglas' arm as they negoti-ated the narrow stairway to the sand below. "Can I ask you a few more questions?" Douglas didn't know what she could possible want to know, but he agreed. "Did you like being married?" He glanced her way, "Yes, I did, but it only lasted two years." She clutched his arm a little tighter. "Think you'll do it again?" Douglas stopped walking. "I think so. You want an on-line dating answer?" She nodded yes. "Yes, if I found the right person. Doesn't that sound like an on-line dating answer?"

They stepped off the stairway onto the sand and Devin steadied herself as she removed her high heels. She continued to hold on to Douglas as they walked a few steps on the cool sand. "You're right. It's the perfect answer for an on-line or blind date. Who would say yes, if I met the wrong person?" They both laughed at that comment. Douglas looked over at his partner as they continued to stroll on the cool sand. "This is nice. Thank you for joining me tonight. Did you see the look on Tony's face when he saw you?" "Yes. He thought I was Marge." Douglas told her that he always came here alone. If Marge finds out I brought you, she will be teasing me about tonight for a long time." She reached down and touched the water, "Well, then thanks again for the invite. Now, I feel very special." They walked quietly for a few moments listening to the surf.

Devin broke the silence, "You know where I live, what about you?" He told her about his condo in West L.A. "I've owned it for the past few years." "Remember, when I get my car, I'm taking you out to one of my favorite places." Douglas smiled, "I'm looking forward to it."

Devin was really enjoying her outing but knew it was time for them to go. "I'm sorry to see this end, but I have designs to finish." Douglas reluctantly agreed, "Yeah, I guess we should go." Douglas took Devin's arm as they walked slowly back to the stairway. She leaned against the handrail for a moment, as she dusted off the sand and slipped into her shoes. She stumbled slightly as they started up the stairs. Douglas caught her. "Have I told you, thanks again, for everything?" Douglas laughed, "About a thousand times. I'm just glad it's all working out for you!"

They finished their climb to the upper parking lot. The valet opened the passenger door, and Devin insisted on tipping the operator. Douglas smiled as they turned toward Silver Lake. During the drive, Devin asked another million questions. "How long have you been a lawyer? What do you do in your off time?" She went on and on. Douglas didn't mind the barrage of questions because it had been a long time since someone was interested enough to ask about him. When they pulled up to her building, he saw that her apartment was lit up. "Did you leave all the lights on?" Devin thought and then said, "No, I didn't. Will you come up for a moment?" "Sure, let's go!"

As they approached the apartment they heard super-loud Latin music. Devin started to unlock the door, but it was already open. She and Douglas entered the apartment to find Shelly dancing in the kitchen. She saw them and yelled, "¡HOLA, Señor y Señorita. Welcome to my cantina!" Devin yelled back, "Ah, hi Shelly, what are you doing?" Shelly dipped the music volume. "I'm making Margaritas! "I have a commercial audition tomorrow." She handed each of them a drink. They cautiously took a sip as Shelly danced around them singing, "What do you think?" They thought the drinks were good. "Very tasty!"

Shelly stopped dancing and looked at Douglas. "Hey, you're the guy who came over." Devin took her arm and escorted her to a chair. "Yes he is; this is Douglas." Devin turned her back to Shelly, "Thank you for dinner and everything." He smiled and told the girls that he had to be running along. He looked toward Shelly, "It was nice seeing you again, Señorita. Goodnight Devin and an early Happy Valentines' Day, ladies!" Devin hugged him and waved her rose at him as he turned to leave. Douglas left the building and smiled all the way home.

Shelly stood and made her way to the makeshift bar. "So, you and, ah…" Devin completed her sentence, "Douglas." "So, you and Douglas had dinner and...?" Devin put her glass on the bar. "And? And, what? We came home to find you dancing in my kitchen. Douglas is the guy that introduced me to the design house. He's not interested in me. He thinks he's too old for me." Shelly picked up two drinks. "I forgot to say congratulations on landing the job. Shall we drink on it? And here's a flash for you. He *is* interested in you. He's not too old for you, you're too old for him." Devin looked at her slightly tipsy friend, "What the heck does that mean?" Shelly licked the last half-inch of salt from her glass,

"He's interested in you, but you don't see it because you act like an old lady all the time. You don't have much fun, you don't open cans of cat food; you don't go dancing or go to dinner with sexy guys like I do. At twenty-eight, you're just an old fogey."

Devin smiled and took another sip. "Hey, this really is good." She stopped drinking and looked at her friend, "Alright, I agree, I'm not the life-of-the-party type. That's where you come in." Shelly nodded in agreement and sucked the last few drops from her glass.

"Shelly, if you don't get the commercial you should apply for a job as a bartender. They make lots of tips. How many different drinks do you know how to make?" Shelly thought for a moment, "Just this one." She directed Devin's attention to the other side of the kitchen.

The sink and counters were loaded with half-empty glasses, cut limes & salt everywhere. Shelly stumbled a little as she said, "I've also been drinking a lot!!!" Devin settled into the couch. "Do you really think he likes me?" Shelly plopped down next to her. "Well, that's a big DUH. I could tell in about five-seconds that he's very interested in you." "Really? How could you tell?" Shelly licked some salt from Devin's glass. "Well, you're both unattached, you're both tall and he couldn't keep his eyes off you. Where did you go tonight?" Devin looked at her rose. "We went to The Italian Grotto in Malibu. It's very nice there." Shelly seemed to know the place. "That's a very high-end, romantic restaurant. I'll bet that's where he takes all of his dates." Devin took another sip. "No, I'm the first person he's ever taken there. Even the owner was shocked to see him with a guest."

Shelly slid off the couch and finished her drink. "Then that clinches it. He likes you. I better go. I gotta be up early for my audition. Goodnight. I'll clean up tomorrow." Devin followed her to the door. "You really think so, huh?" Shelly was about to close the door but stopped to say, "Yes, how many times are you going to ask? Goodnight." Devin leaned into the hallway. "Are you sure?" Shelly quietly yelled. "Yes, a thousand times, yes! Goodnight!" Devin was smiling broadly. "Well, alright then." She looked around her messy kitchen. "If I ever start a bar I know who to hire as a bartender, but not as a maid."

Chapter 5

New Suit Day

Monday, March 7th

Douglas arrived early at the office. He was so early that Marge wasn't there, yet. *"Oh, this is good,"* he thought. *"I'll just wait and when she gets here, I'll pop out of nowhere."* He saw the elevator arriving at the 7th floor, so he hurried to Marge' desk. The doors opened and Mr. Lawson stepped into the hallway. He seemed shocked to see Douglas, "You're in early. I wish everyone had your drive." Douglas smiled at the comment, "Thank you, sir, I have an early meeting with B & B Fashions about their expansion." Mr. Lawson was happy to hear that the expansion was going well. "Can we talk about the Dennison account a little later?" Douglas said he'd call as soon as he wrapped the morning meeting. Mr. Lawson started down the hallway and turned back to say, "Good! Call when you're free. Nice suit, by the way."

Douglas smiled as he turned around and ran into Marge already at her desk. "How long have you been here?" Marge gave him a non-committal look, "Long enough. Why, is this new suit day?" Douglas turned toward his office, "I just thought I should look nice for our meeting today, that's all." Marge thought he looked nice, "That suit makes you look taller." Douglas wanted to know when the consultants were coming in. Marge checked her watch, "They should be here soon." She handed him files for the meeting and asked if they should move the meeting to the small conference room? Douglas thought that was a good idea. "Have the consultants set up in there."

Douglas took a few notes for the meeting while he waited. When everyone from B & B arrived, they were taken to the conference room. Douglas entered the room with Marge not far behind. He introduced Susan & Bart from Alpha Consulting to everyone in the room. "This is Bernice & Bernie of B & B Fashions." Bernie acknowledged the introduction and said, "This is Devin Clark, one of our new designers." Marge was shocked at this introduction. She looked at Douglas, who was smiling and she scribbled something on her pad and turned it so Douglas could read it. "**Now I know why you wore the new suit**."

Douglas smiled as he welcomed everyone, "I'm glad you're all here. I want to turn the floor over to Susan and Bart for a moment and let them tell you how they think you should proceed. Bart?" Bart and Susan presented their concept. They illustrated everything using a computer model. They showed B & B their idea for the website. They also indicated some marketing techniques that could be used and generally set the groundwork for the new wing of B & B fashions.

Douglas thanked Susan and Bart and wondered if there were any questions. Bernie looked totally overwhelmed and wanted to know if all that stuff was written down? Susan handed him a file containing everything they covered. Bernice was also a little confused by everything that was presented. "There are a lot of things we have to do." Douglas assured them that they didn't have to do everything at once. "We can build it piece-by-piece."

Douglas turned to Devin. "Do you have any thoughts or questions?" Devin asked if all their designs would go on the website. Susan said, "Not all of them right now, just a few, to give the over-all look at the line. Then later, when you produce a runway show, everything from the show will be featured on the site." Devin thanked her, "That makes sense."

The meeting concluded with everyone agreeing on just about everything that was presented. B & B would get the designs and photos to the website people as soon as possible. When the room was clear, Marge and Douglas started picking up cups, etc. Marge grinned at him. "So, that was your dinner date?" Douglas frowned at her and said, "Business, I told you." Marge opened the trash bag and held it out to Douglas. She winked at him and said, "When someone is that pretty and tall, it's *not just* business." Douglas leaned on the conference table. "Wait a minute, how did you know we went to dinner?" Marge gave him an evil glare as she said, "I got a call from Tony about the contracts and one thing led to another." Douglas realized he had no secrets. "Marge, she's only twenty-eight."

Marge couldn't believe what he said, "Are you're saying she's too young for you?" Douglas closed the trash bag. "You don't think so?" She grabbed the bag from him, glared at him and said, "You are the biggest stick in the mud I've ever met. Did you see the way she was looking at you during the meeting?" He didn't. Marge opened the door and looked back at Douglas. "Well, that's part of the problem. I think the girl likes you. Lord knows why, but she does."

When Marge left the room, Douglas made a call, "Hi Devin. How do you think it went?" She thought the presentation was great. He was happy to hear that. "They said you were their new designer. So, I guess you got the job?" She laughed and told him, "No, but they probably didn't want to say our apprentice designer. If I really had the job, you would have been the first to know." He wondered if there was any word on her car repairs. She told him it would be ready next week. "So, I'll be calling you for that dinner I owe you." He ended the call and stepped into the hallway. He stopped and looked around to see if anyone was around. "Marge, you think she really likes me?" She looked at him and let out a gasp of air, "Men are so dense sometimes that they miss the obvious!" He turned towards his office smiling, "Okay, I'll take your word for it."

He stopped and asked if she had made reservations for the corporate meeting. Marge told him, "You know I did. You have a non-smoking mini-suite." He asked if she was planning on going. It never occurred to her to attend. Douglas thought for a moment and said, "Well, plan on it. Bring your husband too. Everything is on me. Put your room on my account and then charge all your food to the room."

Marge was suddenly very happy. "Really? Ralph's going to be excited!" Douglas smiled too, "It's my gift to you and Ralph. But, you'll have to come to the banquet and hear the boring speeches." She joked with him, "All right, we'll suffer through it. I'll set everything up. Thank you." Douglas turned back toward his glass prison as he called it. "My pleasure. I like being in Anaheim, even for meetings; it makes me feel like I'm on vacation."

Marge went back to her desk, excited about the trip. She called Ralph who loved the idea. She started making their hotel reservations. Douglas and Mr. Lawson spent a few minutes discussing the Dennison account. "I want you to second-chair with me on this." Douglas agreed and realized that he would really be busy now!

The day was winding down as Douglas found himself thinking more and more about a certain fledgling fashion designer. He wondered why he met her now, instead of eleven years ago. Then he realized with a chuckle, that she would have been under age. Douglas really felt that an eleven-year difference was too much. She needed someone younger.

Chapter 6

Get A Life

Today, when Douglas dragged himself to the office, he found a wrapped package on his desk. The card read, "To Douglas - from Marge & Ralph." He loved presents and let out a big laugh when he opened this one. It was a desk plaque that said, **"GET A LIFE."** *"Truer words were never spoken,"* he thought as he joined Marge at her desk. "Thank you for the laugh and the plaque; it's just what I needed."

She smiled, "We thought so. You've been burning the candle three ways lately. Ralph says thanks for inviting us on the corporate weekend." She checked her note pad. "I have a meeting about our new computer system soon. You can join us, but since I'm the one who will set it up, run it and then upload the reports to the billing department, you won't get much out of the lecture." Douglas was way too busy to be going to a meeting about a computer program anyway.

Marge returned in about an hour with a stack of books and notes. She piled them on his desk. "All this is about how the new computer system works. I don't expect you to read any of them because you have work to do. Here are six files for you to review. Each should take only ten minutes. See you in one hour. I'll hold all calls." "Thank you. Marge, what would I do without you?" She laughed, "I've been asking myself that question for 12 years. As she reached the door he asked, "What is the answer?" She just shook her head.

The day dragged by and Douglas was starting to feel the long hours. Seeing Marge preparing to leave for the day, He looked at his new desk plaque and considered taking off too. He entered the hallway. She looked at him, "Oh, don't tell me you're going home?" He said he was feeling a little tired. She picked up her purse. "You'd really be tired if you had to learn the new computer system." Douglas had a question, "Did you say you've been working with me for twelve years?" She turned off her desk lamp. "Yes, twelve very looooong years." Douglas couldn't believe it. "Well, you've kept me computer-free all that time. For that, I thank you!" She wondered if he would ever consider opening his own firm. Douglas pointed toward his office. "What? And leave all this? Never happen. But, if I go anywhere, you'll be part of the deal."

They headed down the hall toward the elevator. Marge wanted to know if he'd talked to Devin Clark lately. "She seems like such a nice girl." He agreed. "Yes, a very nice young lady and very talented too!" Marge pushed the down button. "Working long hours like you do, you don't get to meet many or *any* nice girls for that matter." Douglas said, "True, and when I do, they're too young." Marge pushed the down button again. "Did she say that?" He didn't want to answer but he did, "No. But Marge, it's an eleven-year difference. I think that's too much."

The elevator doors opened. She entered first and gave him a piece of her mind. "Look, if you like her, and I think you do, you should let her make up her own mind about that. He smiled at her, "Thank you, Matchmaker, but in all these years, how many relationships have I been able to maintain?" Marge let him have it again, "None! But this is different! She's not like the others. She has goals! She's working toward owning her own company!" He didn't say anything as the elevator voice said, "Parking Lot A." As the doors opened he said, "I gotta go, too much of the Doctor Marge Show."

They stepped out of the elevator. "Goodnight Douglas. Oh, did you see the memo that the conference dates have been changed?" He stopped and looked at her with a puzzled stare. "I didn't think you saw it. They moved it to April 16. That's the day after somebody's Birthday. I rescheduled all the reservations. We're all set for the Anaheim Conference. My husband is very excited!" Douglas started toward his car. "So, you can plan this like a second honeymoon for yourself." Marge grinned, "No, he's excited because he hasn't been to an amusement park in years." Douglas laughed as he said, "Goodnight Marge, see you tomorrow. Thanks again for the plaque." She walked toward her car and yelled, "Call her, Douglas, say hi at least. If she's working as much as you, she probably could use a friendly hello." Douglas yelled back, "Goodnight Doctor."

He watched as Marge drove out of the garage. He then, placed a call but he had to leave a message. "*Hi Devin. Douglas here. Just wanted to call to see how things were going with you. Give me a call when you have time.*" He entered his car, put the briefcase and phone on the passenger seat and the GPS lady said "Hello, where would you like to go? Douglas said one word. "Home." He put the car in gear and drove off toward the nice California sunset, and The Village Tavern.

Chapter 7

Rubber Chicken & Speeches

March went out like a lion. In the last week of the month, Douglas had court appearances, two major contract disputes and countless phone calls. Now, with the awards conference just two days away, many in the office were trying to wrap up business and file taxes so they could leave without things hanging over their heads.

Douglas was well on his way to the top of the billable-hours list again. He was looking forward to the conference, the awards banquet and of course the bonus check. He was ready for the trip to Anaheim. He asked if everything was set for the weekend. Marge ran down her list. "Yes, I've checked all the reservations for the hotel and the banquet, we're good to go, and since the B & B expansion is about ninety-five percent finished, you can relax a little."

Marge started to leave but stopped, "Speaking of B & B, have you talked to Devin lately?" Douglas told her they had been playing phone tag for almost a month. Marge told him to keep trying, "Oh…forgot to mention I booked you two extra nights. I know you don't like to hear this, but Happy Birthday!" Douglas picked up a pen to make a note on his desk calendar.

"You're right! I don't like to hear that. But thank you. So, I'm there today, Saturday, Sunday and Monday?"

Marge checked her schedule. "You won't be back here until Tuesday. I set it up that way because you need some time away." Douglas looked around his office to make sure he had everything he would need. "I think you're right. Okay, I'm outta here!" She watched him leave and had to ask, "Where's your suitcase?" Douglas pushed the down button. "It's in the car. I'll see you there about 5-ish?" Marge told him they would be there later than that because her husband had to work till five. He held the door open. "Okay, see you later. Let's have dinner tonight at the hotel. Call me when you get in." The doors closed and Douglas thought, *"I can't believe she booked me two extra days, I'm really going on a vacation!"*

The drive to Anaheim wasn't very busy for a Friday. He pulled up to Valet Parking in front of the hotel. The bellman took his bag and he walked directly to the desk. All they needed was his name since Marge had everything arranged. The hotel rep handed him two key cards and a coaster that was good for a free drink at the lobby bar. "Hope you'll have a wonderful stay with us." Douglas smiled and was about to ask where the bar was when he saw it across from the restaurant. He entered and the bartender asked what Douglas would like to drink. He flashed the coaster and said, "Gin and Tonic, please." He looked around, didn't see anybody else from the firm, so he moved to one of the large arm chairs in the corner, undid his tie, and seemed to relax for the first time in a very long time. He watched the sports channel for a few minutes, finished his drink then wandered into the lobby and stopped at the dining room to look at their menu.

The attentive hostess asked if he'd be dining with them this evening. "Yes, I think so." She told him that the restaurant gets busy at dinner time. "Don't wait too long to make a reservation. We have a wonderful buffet." Douglas thanked her for the suggestion, "Table for three at six-thirty - Thank you."

Douglas headed up to his spacious 12th floor mini-suite with two queen-size beds and a nice lanai. He hung up a few shirts and relaxed for a moment in the living room area, watching the large-screen TV. He picked up a tie and started thinking about getting dressed for dinner. That's when it hit him that he was sort-of on vacation. He dumped his tie and suit as he looked over the outfits he brought.

After a shower and shave Douglas slipped into an understated short-sleeve resort shirt. It's was a great look for someone on vacation. Back in the lobby, he checked the time on his cell phone, and asked the concierge if Marge and her husband had arrived. "Not yet," said the young lady at the front desk. "I think your phone is ringing." Douglas thanked her and answered the call. "Hello this is Douglas Hedges."

The friendly voice on the phone was Devin. She apologized for playing phone tag with him. "Where are you?" He told her he was in Anaheim and was about to mention the conference when Devin said, "That's right. I spoke with Marge she told me about the conference, your birthday and your award so, I just had to call and congratulate you and say Happy Birthday!" Douglas returned to the same chair he had earlier in the lobby bar. "Thank you. Fill me in, what have you been up to?"

Douglas motioned to the bartender as he talked to Devin who told him about her very busy schedule working on a lot of new designs. She also went into some detail about B & B's upcoming fashion show. "I'll tell you all about it, when you get back. I gotta run now, I'm working all weekend again. Talk to you soon."

Douglas suddenly felt a lot better. He used the house phone to ask the desk to call him in the bar when Marge checked-in. The bartender placed a bowl of pretzels on the small table next to his armchair and asked if he wanted another drink. He, of course, said yes as he took a few munchies. It was after six when the desk alerted him that Marge and Ralph had arrived. Douglas selected a table in the buffet restaurant and sent Marge a text telling her where to meet him. He had another drink while he waited. Dinner with Marge and Ralph was nice. He told them about Devin's call and Marge told him she liked his subtle tropical look.

Ralph said he bought them two-day passes for the amusement park. They were going early Saturday to join a Character Breakfast. Douglas had to agree that going to the park was more fun than hanging around the hotel. Marge said, "Yes, it is. The conference talks are usually a snore-fest. Don't worry we'll be back in-time for cocktails and dinner." Marge placed a cupcake in front of Douglas. "Here's your birthday cake. Notice no candles. This way, nobody will know."

Douglas raised the tasty treat. "Thank you for the mini birthday cake and for coming along this weekend." Ralph thanked Douglas for inviting them. "I've been working long hours on a new construction job, and really needed a few days off. Plus, I haven't been to the park in about 15 years. I'm looking forward to seeing all the new stuff." Marge and Ralph needed to get to bed for their early morning outing. Douglas decided to spend some time in the lobby bar, before turning-in.

The friendly voice on the phone said, "Good morning, it's seven AM sir." Time to get up and get going Douglas thought. *"Now, for the decision of the day, what should I wear to the conference? A suit? No! A casual look would be best. I'll wear a suit tonight for the banquet."* He selected a normal business shirt and slacks, and headed for breakfast. Once inside the main lobby restaurant, his morning coffee in-hand, he felt better, but as usually happens at a buffet, he couldn't make up his mind what he wanted to eat.

Across the lobby he saw Marge and waved to catch her attention. Douglas moved to the front of the restaurant. "Sorry you can't join me for breakfast." Ralph said they were eating at the park. Marge noticed the shuttle pull up in front of the hotel. "Let's go, we'll see you tonight."

Douglas waved as Marge headed for a day of fun in the sun. He finished his breakfast, the newspaper, and checked email on his cell phone before heading toward the conference. The morning session dragged on as did lunch and the afternoon session as well. The topics were well-suited for younger, first-year lawyers. Douglas didn't need to know how to bill more hours. He was thinking during that talk, *"If I booked any more hours, I would have to put a bed and TV in my office and just live there."* Douglas swore it was nine PM when it finished, but it was only three o'clock. Time to dress for tonight, now he was happy he had extra time away from the office.

He picked up a brochure in the lobby about the amusement park and was thinking about getting a one-day pass for Sunday. *"That's an idea,"* he thought, as he headed to the 12th floor to get dressed for the big awards banquet.

The invitation said…
6 PM - Cocktails and Hors d'oeuvres
7 PM Dinner
8 PM Awards Program
9 PM - 12 Midnight Dancing

Douglas liked the schedule and hoped that Marge could dance. He thought, *"I've known the woman for over twelve years and I don't even know if she can cha-cha."* The cocktail party was in full-swing when Douglas arrived. Lots of pats-on-the-back and congrats toasts. Marge and Ralph showed up, a little sunburned, but full of smiles. Douglas looked at the red-faced couple. "I assume that today was hot and fun, right?" His right-hand lady said, "Yes, it was both and very crowded! I could use a drink and a chair." She grabbed Ralph's arm, "What's our table number?" Douglas said, "Three".

Marge and Ralph headed off into the ballroom as Douglas finished his drink and finger food. He asked the waiter to come to table three. He wanted to buy drinks for everyone. Going around the table he saw

Marge, Ralph, Miss Shilling and her fiancé, Mr. Christopher and his wife and the eighth chair was empty. The DJ was playing some nice dinner jazz in the background. Douglas pointed to the empty chair, "Who will be sitting there?" Marge told him that she invited her sister to join them. "I told her that she should meet the best boss in the world." Douglas was flattered. Mr. Lawson was smiling as he made the rounds of the tables. "Welcome everyone! I hope you have a great time tonight."

Douglas proposed a toast to the other top billers at the table. He turned to Marge, "I don't think I've met any of your family before. I'm looking forward to meeting your sister." Marge smiled and said, "Good, then turn around."

Douglas turned to see Devin standing in the doorway. She entered the ballroom wearing a red off-the-shoulder, medium-length evening dress. It seemed like she had practiced her runway walk, because she floated across the room to table three. All eyes were on Douglas as he stood to greet her. For a moment, it was just like *"Julia Roberts in Pretty Woman."* She looked that good! Devin hugged Douglas then greeted Marge and her husband.

Marge introduced her to the others at the table because Douglas was speechless. Marge leaned over towards him to whisper, "You're smiling again." Douglas pulled out the extra chair for Devin. "Well, to say I'm surprised is the understatement of the century. I thought you were working today." The waiter arrived and poured wine for everyone.

Devin took a sip. "I did work today from nine till three and now it's evening and I'm not working. And neither are you!" She took Douglas' cell phone and put it on the table. Douglas looked at the phone, "You're right. I'm not working tonight. None of us are." The other two lawyers agreed and put their phones on the table too. Everyone did a group toast to not working tonight! Douglas reached across the table to shake the hands of the other lawyers. He said, "Let's all turn off our phones." They all raised the units and pushed the off button together. Marge said, "Now, all of you are really on vacation."

Douglas explained to Devin that the other two attorneys were high on the list for awards tonight. "And, we're all on vacation!" Everyone cheered. Marge said, "This is going to be a better party than I expected. Douglas, what if you didn't bill sixty-five-plus hours a week. What would happen?" Douglas glared at her, "Marge, bite your tongue"

Marge kept going, "I'm just saying, if you ever got a private life, you wouldn't end up booking so many hours in a month. You couldn't!" Douglas looked around the table and felt he should explain what was going on. "Marge has been my right & left arm for over 12 years. She and Ralph gave me a gift. It's a desk plaque that says, GET A LIFE!" The table erupted in laughter and light applause for Marge who had to respond, 'But if he got married, you know he'd want to get home early." Douglas leaned over to Marge. "You know I can hear you. I'm sitting right here and I'm listening." She starred him down, "I know you're listening, but I don't know if you're really hearing me."

Mr. Christopher jumped in to try to help the conversation. "I wish my assistant was as nice as yours, Douglas." Douglas laughed and said, "Marge is a sweetheart, most of the time." She tried to change the subject. "Devin I'm glad you could make it." The young designer was laughing as she said, "Marge, you guys really crack me up, it's like you're married, but you're not." Devin sensed that Ralph was a little uncomfortable with the topic. "Ralph, I didn't mean they were really married, but after twelve years together, they just seem joined at the hip."

The quiet background music faded out and the voice over announcer said, "Dinner is being served, enjoy!" The waiters began to place the dinner plates at each table setting. Everyone began to eat; it was a good dinner, not rubber chicken, for sure! Mr. Christopher asked Devin how long she'd known Douglas. "I met him about three months ago, right after New Year's. I just got hired by one of his clients, B & B fashions." Douglas played press-agent and told everybody about his very talented designer friend who someday would have her own line of fashions.

Devin smiled and took his hand. "You really think so?" Douglas had a sip of wine, "How does Devin Designs sound?" "That's what my business card says, so of course it sounds great; I like it, why?" He took another sip of wine. "I'm glad you like it because I already set up the website for you. It's created and waiting for your designs." She was very excited. "You really did that?" He nodded yes and she gave him a fist bump.

The dinner concluded with a wonderful dessert and coffee. The ladies excused themselves to visit the powder room. Devin stopped, came back to the table and picked up Douglas' cell phone. "You're on vacation, remember?"

While the girls were gone, Ralph and Douglas talked about his work in construction and how during his busy season he was never around either. Douglas learned that Marge and Ralph had a twenty-fifth wedding anniversary coming up soon. The ladies returned just as the lights dimmed in the room. Mr. Lawson took the stage and adjusted the microphone.

The owner of the company welcomed everyone to the annual awards presentation. "I hope you enjoyed today's conference and I hope you got some ideas for the future". The audience applauded the statement. Mr. Lawson talked for about thirty-minutes mentioning the firm's current business and the fact that the second quarter was off to a great start. He said the future looked bright for everyone. Finally, it was award time. He called Mr. Christopher & Miss Shilling to the stage and then brought Douglas up.

Mr. Lawson handed a plaque to each of the law-yers. Some snapped a few photos and then he asked Douglas to say a few words. Douglas moved to the small podium. "Thank you, Mr. Lawson. Congratulations to Mr. Christopher and Miss Shilling and to all the members of the firm. The best part of the night is yet to come, the bonus checks! Thank you all." Mr. Lawson held up a stack of envelops and said he'd be around to see everyone. "So, don't leave early and do enjoy the rest of your evening."

Everyone left the stage as the lighting in the room changed and the dance floor displayed pools of colored light. The soft dance music began. Douglas made his way back to table three. He leaned his award on a wine bottle as Devin and Marge gave him make-believe applause. Douglas smiled as he asked, "Who wants to dance? Marge raised her drink, "Not me, I've been on my feet too much today!" Douglas looked at Devin, "Do you dance?" She grabbed his hand as she said, "I'd love to dance. I was a ballroom dance instructor for a year after college."

Douglas smiled as she dragged him to the dance floor. Marge sat back with Ralph and watched as Douglas took the lady in red in his arms for the slow foxtrot. "This is nice, thanks for coming." Devin held on to her friend, "I wouldn't have missed it for anything." He held her and asked if she would tell him the Devin story. "You were a dance teacher and?" She hugged him, "Not now, let's just dance." Douglas smiled a little, "All right, but you owe me a story." She looked at him, "You owe me *your* full story too." They continued to dance the medium-tempo foxtrot holding each other close - for the first time. It was a nice moment. The song ended and a med-tempo cha-cha started.

Devin smiled and said, "Oh, a cha-cha, okay?" Her partner smiled back and said, "Sure, I like Latin dances." Douglas, as she soon learned, was a very good dancer. He had a smooth, professional style. Marge was watching and couldn't believe it. Devin was impressed too. She said, "Okay, no story now, but do tell me why you dance so well?" Douglas broke from her and did a few solo steps. "Well, you taught ballroom for a year, I taught it for four years. I've won two dance championships!" Devin did a few twirls. "I never would have guessed that one. Now you really owe me the full story." They finished the cha-cha and walked to the table as a nice waltz started. Marge applauded the dancers. "Wow that was really great! I didn't know you could do that Douglas. You have hidden talents."

She grabbed her husband. "It's a slow one, we're going to dance one now." Marge and Ralph danced the waltz and then sat down again to watch all the dance floor action. Devin dragged Douglas back on to the floor for a rumba. She said, "I hope you rumba."

Douglas twirled her and held her super-close, "Hope you can keep up." They looked great on the floor. It had been a long time since Douglas had so much fun. "I haven't been dancing in years." Devin pulled him close as she said, "Neither have I; we'll have to do it again sometime. Douglas thought that was a great idea.

The night continued with Mr. Lawson making the rounds, handing out checks, taking photos with his associates and of course dancing. He finished his "rounds" at table three and said goodnight to Marge and everyone. "I didn't know Douglas was such a good dancer," he said as he and his wife decided to do the last dance. The DJ announced, "This will be our final dance of the evening" as he started The Love Unlimited Orchestra's instrumental version of "Love's Theme." Douglas held out his hand, "Last dance." Devin took his hand, "Last chance."

Marge & Ralph and a few others joined Douglas and Devin on the dance floor. The pair was moving slowly to the music and Douglas was beginning to realize that he had very strong feelings for this young lady. He wondered how many other things they had in common, as he held her tightly. Devin looked at Douglas knowing that she hadn't felt like this about anyone in a very long time. She also knew that he felt he was too old for her. It was time to change his thinking.

Devin put her head on her partner's shoulder. "Devin, you seem a bit tired. Are you sure you can drive home?" She told him that she was okay. Douglas danced near Marge, "I don't know if Devin should drive home tonight, she seems a little tired." They stopped dancing and moved to their table. Marge asked how she was feeling. Devin said she was a little dizzy. Marge knew Devin had wine with dinner. "Maybe you shouldn't drive home tonight. Can you stay over?" Devin said, "I don't have a meeting until tomorrow at six, so I could stay." Marge was ready with an answer, "Douglas, you have two beds in your room."

Douglas was shocked at the thought but said, "Yes, I do have a suite, with two beds. You're welcome to stay there, if you like." Devin looked up at her dance partner, "You really wouldn't mind?" Marge butted-in again, "I think that's a good idea." Devin kiddingly looked at Marge and asked, "You think I can trust this guy?" Marge sat next to Devin and quietly said, "Here's one thing I know for sure. This guy is very trustworthy. If he gives you any trouble, call me." She grabbed Ralph, "We gotta get to bed. The sun really knocked us out today!"

As they walked away Douglas said, "Marge, glad you folks came. Enjoy the rest of your short break. Have breakfast in the room tomorrow." Devin said, "Goodnight, Marge, Ralph, I'll see you in the morning, I guess?" The music ended. Douglas collected his plaque and Devin picked up her large purse, her wrap and program. He said goodnight to Mr. Lawson and they crossed the lobby to the elevators.

Inside the twelfth-floor suite, Douglas put his things down on the coffee table. Both beds had been turned down and there was a small orchid and wrapped chocolate on each pillow. Devin opened her purse and returned his cell phone which he plugged in. She pointed toward the beds. "May I?" Douglas, who couldn't believe what was going on said, "Take your pick! If you want something to sleep in, there are robes and slippers in the closet. Relax and have some candy. There's a flower too."

He gave her an orchid from the pillow and turned on the TV's relaxation music station, and said, "I'll be out in a moment," as he entered the bathroom. He was finding it hard to believe what had happened tonight. Devin showing up, his very large bonus check and now this! He washed his hands, brushed his teeth and left the bathroom to find Devin fast-asleep on top of the sheets.

Douglas used a small blanket from the closet to cover her. He turned down the lights, left the music playing softly, took off his shoes and quietly stretched out on the other bed. He whispered, "Goodnight Devin." Douglas looked across at his beautiful friend and smiled, as he too closed his eyes. *It's been a most unusual day!*

Chapter 8

The Morning After

Douglas didn't sleep much. He kept waking up every few hours and looking over to make sure Devin was all right. She was fine. He looked at the digital clock on the night stand. It showed, 6:30 AM. He slid off his bed trying not to make noise and moved to the lanai. He turned on his cellphone to see if he had any urgent messages. There weren't any. Devin opened her eyes, looked at the surroundings, and after realizing that she slept in her party dress, she remembered what happened.

Douglas noticed she was awake. "Good morning, young lady, how did you sleep?" She sat up against the headboard. "I slept in my clothes! What time did I nod off?" Douglas told her that she fell asleep as soon as they got in the room. "You slept like a baby and you didn't snore much." Devin laughed and asked if she could use the bathroom. "Sure, the hotel provides tooth brushes, tooth paste, shower gel, a hair dryer and everything else you need. Go ahead."

Devin grabbed her over-sized purse and made her way to the bathroom. Douglas read the coffee maker instructions and asked if she wanted some? He added two cups of water and then pushed the red button. As he finished making a second cup, he heard a sound in the hall. Someone slid the Sunday paper under the door. Douglas took his coffee and the newspaper to the lanai. He sat, looked out at the morning and wondered what kind of day it was going to be. So far, it was pretty good! Devin finished in the bathroom and joined Douglas on the lanai. She was wearing a colorful t-shirt and jeans.

"Where did you get those clothes?" She took her cup of coffee, "It's what I wore yesterday when I drove down here. I put them in my purse. You didn't think I drove in my evening gown, did you?" Douglas smiled back at his overnight guest, "Well, that's called creative thinking; how's your coffee?" "It's okay. Thank you for letting me stay here last night. I guess I was extremely tired." Douglas smiled at her, "No, that wasn't you being tired! You were just proving that I'm the most boring guy in the room." She told him that wasn't the reason, "I've been working very hard, and needed the rest." He picked up a room card from the table. "How about going to the hotel's Sunday Champagne Breakfast? I owe you food for all the great dancing." She told him she'd love to and politely ordered him to, "Get dressed."

Douglas was smiling a lot as he shaved and dressed for his Sunday Vacation. He and Devin entered the hotel's main restaurant and were seated at a nice table in the back. The waiter brought them coffee, flutes of Champagne and orange juice to start. Douglas said, "Let's just drink a little and relax; we're both on vacation! She disagreed, "No, you're on vacation. I have to go to work today." She paused and looked at him, "Okay, you're on, go." He starred at her as if she was nuts, "What?" She told him she wanted to hear the full Douglas Hedges story.

Douglas began to give her a few highlights from his very normal life. His first job was at a fast-food restaurant which was owned by a lawyer. That's what started him thinking about law as a career. During college, he worked as a part-time dance instructor and still made high grades.

His mom & dad and brother lived on the West Coast, but he only saw them on holidays. He'd been a lawyer for about 14 years and at his current job for five. He told her he had a big client load and worked non-stop. Because of his work schedule, he hardly ever got a chance to go to movies, concerts or do much.

"Many of my clients give me free passes to events all the time, and usually, I can't attend." He mentioned that he used to play golf, many years back, but he hadn't played in years. He keeps thinking about going to the gym, but never seems to find the time. "Well, as you can see, my story isn't that exciting." She wasn't buying it. "I wouldn't say that. You're a very stable person, who's honest and trustworthy. That's why I stayed over last night. Marge said you could be trusted. After we eat, how about we just relax by the indoor pool?" Douglas thought that was a great idea. "But food first."

As they looked over the wonderful breakfast buffet layout she told him she wanted to show him her new designs and her new car. He asked for a custom-made omelet and said, "Great idea, after food." Douglas spotted Marge & Ralph out of the corner of his eye. Marge joined them just long enough to say they were leaving early. "Ralph wants to go back to the park for a few hours." She hugged Devin and was happy she joined them last night. Devin was glad she could get away. "Thanks for telling me about the banquet." Marge smiled and said, "I'm glad you came, you got a free dinner and breakfast out of the trip and I hope a good night's sleep." She smiled, "Yes, Douglas said I slept like a log."

Douglas looked at Marge, "We're going to hang around the pool today and I get to see some of her new designs." Marge smiled, "I get it; it's a new version of come up and see my etchings! Gotta run, Douglas, I'll see you Tuesday." Douglas & Devin in unison said, "Bye Marge, Ralph." Douglas kept smiling as they returned to their table. He couldn't believe that this beautiful young lady was here, with him. She noticed he wasn't eating. "Why are you smiling?" He quietly said, "I'm just happy you're here." She put a berry on her fork. "Well, when Marge told me about the dinner, I thought I should attend. I'm really sorry I fell asleep so fast, I didn't get to see the suite." Douglas dug into his hand-made omelet. "I'm really sorry that I put you to sleep so fast!" They laughed and finished their breakfast.

They headed to the parking garage to pick up Devin's portfolio from her car. Douglas loved the way the car looked—just like it came from the showroom floor. They exited on the pool level and found the perfect place to sit, relax and do nothing for a while. The couch was comfortable as was the easy chair. The pool attendant asked if they would like something to drink. They both agreed on coffee as Devin opened her portfolio.

She and Douglas looked over the drawings, which were top-notch. They also talked about B & B and her new job. She told him about the fashion show that was coming up, and hoped they would use some of her pieces. "Bernie said he'd be sending you and Marge passes for the affair. You have to come; I won't take no for an answer." Before they knew it, the pool attendant said, "Our Sunday breakfast has ended and the restaurant is now serving lunch."

Douglas checked his watch and realized that they had been talking all morning. Devin closed her portfolio, "I think we should eat again, I'm starved." Douglas helped her up from the lounge chair and said, "Well, I know the remedy for that."

At lunch, they continued to talk, laugh and have a good time, just hanging out. Devin reached over to look at his wristwatch. "I don't want to eat and run, but I have to get back. I have a six o'clock meeting today and another in the morning! Bernice is picking the fashions that will be in the show. I want to make sure some of mine make the cut. Hope you understand." As they walked to the front of the hotel Douglas told her he understood, "I also have work piling up but Marge arranged this little vacation for me because, I've also been working too many hours. I'll be back in the office on Tuesday."

While they waited for her car to be brought around Devin told him she had a good time, "Thank you for everything, especially the dances." Douglas smiled, "I had a fun time too. It's nice to be surprised. Plus, I now know someone who can really dance. I'll see you soon, at the fashion show for sure."

She told him to keep watching his email because the invitation would be coming. The attendant delivered Devin's shiny yellow VW bug. Douglas tipped him, put her portfolio in the rear and helped her into the driver's seat. He told her to drive safely. "Call me when you get to Silver Lake." Devin grabbed Douglas' hand and motioned for him to bend down. She kissed him lightly on the cheek. "I'll call you, bye."

As Douglas watched the yellow VW bug drive away from the hotel, he realized that Devin really did matter to him. He turned to re-enter the hotel and caught a glimpse of himself in the hotel's shiny brass nameplate. It was a reality check! He saw the eleven-year age difference and all of a sudden, he felt it!

He crossed the lobby, entered the bar and ordered a gin and tonic. The first of many, after all he thought, *"I'm on vacation."* The sun was going down and there was a line of cocktail stirrers on the table. Douglas thought he really should eat something, as he stood to exit the bar he received a text message. ***"I'm home, thanks for everything. Had a great time. D***

He closed his cell phone and said to the restaurant hostess. "Table for one please."

Chapter 9

All Work and No Play

Following the conference weekend, Marge noticed that Douglas had slipped right back into his non-stop work routine. He was coming in earlier than normal and leaving after dark which meant he was really racking up the billable hours. The new computer system was working like a charm keeping track of everything and the entire office seemed happy with the results. April blended into May. Douglas had a few text messages from Devin, but never connected on the phone. He realized that he did miss her, but kept coming back to the age-difference.

Marge entered his office holding a print-out. "I just got an email invite to B & B's buyers show. It's on Friday, June seventeenth at six PM. A cocktail reception follows. Should I put it on the calendar?" Douglas thought they both should attend. Marge smiled, "Ok, I'll email them back and I'll tell Ralph I'll be a little late that evening." When he was alone, Douglas sent a text to Devin. *"Just got the invite...Marge and I will be there. See you on 6/17. How many designs will you have in the show?"*

Douglas went back to the computer to make a few client notes. Since everything was now totally automated, he just indicates which client he's working for and their account is charged for his time. Marge was about to leave for the evening when the return text appeared. He read the response to Marge. Devin says, *"I'll see you BOTH on 6/17. Big surprise event! D."* Marge smiled at Douglas, "Oh great, I like surprises. See you tomorrow."

As Marge was shutting down her computer, an email from Bernice arrived. She said she was new at this email stuff and hoped it worked. Bernice asked Marge to call her when she wasn't in the office. She had a question for her. Marge wrote back quickly and said, *"I'll call you tonight!"* Marge left Douglas looking out at the beginning of a beautiful sunset. On a clear day, one could usually see the ocean, but not today.

When Douglas reached his condo that evening he realized that each day since the conference, he wanted to leave work earlier and earlier, but it just didn't happen. He didn't know why he wanted to leave early, because when he was at home, there was really nothing to do. Tonight, he decided to take a walk down to the local shopping area—a cute-looking, upscale section of West L.A. Mostly locals were walking on the tree-lined streets. Many knew each other and exchanged greetings. The glow from the "vintage" street lights added to the quaintness.

Douglas dropped by The Village Tavern which was the "in-spot". The saloon was one of the oldest businesses in the area. Everyone who's anyone dropped by the tavern. Douglas liked to sit at the far end of the bar so he could see the coming and going action. He liked talking to Billy, the bartender, who seemed to know everybody and their stories. "Good evening Douglas, you haven't been around for a while. I thought maybe you got married again." Douglas grabbed a few pretzels from the small bowl as he laughed at Billy's statement. "No Billy, just super busy at work."

The attentive bartender placed a napkin in front of Douglas, "You're a lawyer, and you work in downtown L.A., right?" Douglas congratulated him on his memory. "Yes, it's a long-haul every day. Sometimes the drive takes over an hour. I don't usually mention what I do to anybody, how do you know?" Billy fumbled with some things behind the bar and retrieved Doug's business card. "I keep everything. That's how I remembered. You're right not to mention what you do, because almost everybody wants free advice. You need a drink or two?" Douglas smiled, "Or more." "You're not driving so why not? What'll you have?"

Douglas ordered a gin and lemon-lime soda with lime. "Coming right up!" Douglas sat in his favorite seat and looked around the darkened tavern. He couldn't stop thinking about his crazy weekend. He put his cell phone on the bar as a text message arrived. Billy heard the 'ding' and looked over at Douglas who said, "Always business. I can't escape."

He looked at the text and smiled. *"Doug - I just wanted to say hi, I'm still working. You too? D."* Douglas texted back. *"Home now, see you on 6/17."* He remembered that his phone had a camera. *"I should have taken some shots at the conference,"* he thought. He searched, found the media file and started to look at photos.

#1 - Douglas making his speech
#2 - Devin in her evening dress
#3 - Douglas and Devin dancing

Douglas realized that Marge must have played with his phone in Anaheim. He was glad she did because he felt better just seeing Devin's photo. Deep inside, he really hated the fact that she had made such an impression on him. Was the difference in their age really a problem? Douglas was feeling very confused about everything. He wondered if talking to a professional might help. He'd never done that sort of thing before; he never felt the need. He didn't know anybody who'd ever done that either. He also didn't know anybody he could really talk to. He asked Billy. "Do you know anybody who ever saw a therapist?" Billy grinned at him, "Sure! Plus, I hear problems all day long. I wish they would all go see a therapist."

Douglas finished his drink. "I know, but I wonder if it really does any good?" Billy took his glass and began to make a second drink, "I think it does help. Hey, it can't hurt. If you don't have anybody to talk to, that could be the answer." He put the new gin concoction in front of Douglas. "Dr. Martha is a family therapist. She's in here all the time since her office is just a few doors down. She's has a lot of clients." Douglas quickly finished his drink and told Billy he was heading home. "See you soon."

Douglas exited the bar and strolled slowly down the sidewalk doing some window shopping on the way home. Next to the gourmet bakery he saw a stairway leading to the second floor and a sign, **Dr. Martha English, Family Therapist.** Douglas entered her number in his cell phone. "Free consultation." He was thinking out loud. "Okay, I'll give her a call tomorrow. Lord knows, I can't talk to Marge or I'll never hear the end of it." Douglas smiled as he headed to his condo, feeling a little better.

Marge reached her home and immediately called Bernice. She was very curious about her email. Bernice had noticed that since Devin returned from Anaheim, she was really acting differently. She had been working till all hours and seemed distracted from time-to-time. Bernice said she talked to Devin and thinks she has feelings for Douglas. Marge chuckled, "I think that's all it is. She likes him, but hasn't told him." Bernice agreed and said, "And he likes her, but hasn't said anything. Right?" Marge told Bernice, "Douglas feels he's too old for her. He thinks she should be with a younger guy." Bernice said, "What? That's really silly! Bernie is older than me. Of course, he'd never admit it, but he is."

The ladies decided that they would make it their personal project to get the two of them together. "I'll see you at the fashion show. But don't let on that we talked." Marge agreed and when she hung up the phone, the wheels started turning.

Douglas arrived at the office very tired the next morning, probably because he was out too late at the tavern. He had the therapy doctor's phone number stored in his phone, but he got busy and sort-of forgot about calling. His office load was getting much heavier. He had two court dates scheduled and had to prepare. Even if he did call Dr. Martha, he wouldn't have time to meet with her. There was just too much business and not enough personal time. Marge could see the strain on his face and how tired he was becoming. She asked if he had seen his doctor lately. "I'm worried about how much you've been working." Douglas laughed, "When do I have time to see a doctor? Do you know anyone who has office hours at midnight? That's when I get home."

Marge shook her head and let out a gasp, "No wonder you look tired. Don't forget to bring a change of clothes tomorrow." He didn't understand what she meant. "Tomorrow is B & B's fashion show." He finally got it. "Okay, I will. Please remind me later. Send me a text. I didn't realize it was tomorrow." Douglas was trying to forget about Devin but the more he tried, the more he found himself drifting away thinking about her and wondering what he should do. When he was alone, he picked up his cell and called Dr. Martha English. It rang only once. "This is Dr. English's service. May I have your name and number please? The doctor will return your call ASAP."

Douglas gave her his cell number and told the operator to have the Doctor call any time. Douglas thought, *"We'll see how good she is at returning calls."* Douglas opened a file on his desk and before he could read the second paragraph, his cell phone rang. "Hello, this is Douglas Hedges." It was Dr. English returning his call. Douglas turned his chair toward his city view. "Hello Doctor English. I was walking in the Village last evening and saw your sign. I don't know if what I'm struggling with is something you can address."

Dr. Martha told him, "I usually deal with family matters. Is this a family problem?" Douglas wasn't sure, "I guess it is." The doctor asked if he could give her a quick version of his problem. Douglas explained as fast as he could, "I met a young lady eleven years younger than I am. I'm sort-of in conflict about it because I feel I'm too old for her." The doctor asked, "Did she say that to you?" Douglas said, "No, it's just a feeling I have."

Dr. Martha told him, "Come to the office tonight. I won't be free until eight, but I could talk to you then. It's a free consult." Douglas was all smiles when he said, "All right, I'll be there." He ended the call and told Marge, that he was going to leave at six. "I'll bring a change of clothes for tomorrow." Marge didn't understand. "Are you feeling OK?" Douglas shut down his computer. "I'm fine. I just feel like taking a break." Marge logged off her computer system and she and Douglas walked out together.

Marge couldn't believe it. "Do you realize that this is the first time, in I don't know how many years that we've left the office at the same time?" Douglas knew it had been quite a while. They arrived at their cars and Marge waved, "See you tomorrow. Don't forget your change of clothes."

Douglas drove to his condo relaxed a little and changed into comfortable non-lawyer attire. He put on a light jacket and headed to the village, and ducked into the tavern, just to say hello to Billy and tell him he'd be back later. At seven-forty-five PM he climbed the stairs to Dr. Martha's office, opened the outer door and entered the empty reception area. It was quiet and nicely appointed. Douglas took a seat and noted that he was fifteen minutes early.

At eight PM, the interior door opened and Dr. Martha English entered. She seemed to be a little older than Douglas, but very trim and attractive. She welcomed him, "Good Evening, you must be Mr. Hedges." He took a chair and handed her his business card. "Yes I am." "I'm Martha English. You can see all my certificates on the wall, so you know what I do." She looked at his card. "So, you took the chair on the left counselor?"

Douglas didn't know what to make of her statement. "The chair on the left? Is that significant?" She gave him a sly smile, "No, it's something I saw in a movie once. I always thought it was a good opening line." Douglas laughed and looked around her very impressive office. It resembled a page from a very high-end decorator magazine. She looked at his card again. "So, you're an attorney who works in downtown and you live near here?" He told her he was just a short walk away. "I've been an over-worked lawyer for many years." She thanked him for calling her and asked if she could call him Douglas. "Please do." Dr. Martha got serious, "Tell me about the relationship you mentioned on the phone."

Douglas began to describe his relationship with Devin. He told Doctor Martha how they met, and about the surprise conference weekend with the overnight stay. He mentioned the dancing and how he felt when she left that day. He also said that the age difference was the big stumbling block for him. He talked about his failed marriage and the email from his ex-wife. The Doctor listened intently and took notes as Douglas talked. She looked up from her note pad. "Devin sounds like a fun lady. Do you have a photo?" Douglas searched his phone, "Yes, I do. Marge, my

secretary snapped this during our conference weekend."
He handed her the phone.

"She's beautiful. I think most men wouldn't be here
if that girl was anywhere around them. So?" He didn't
know what to make of her statement. "Oh, there's a so?"
She put her pad and pen on the desk. "Yes, the so
means, you're not most men. You're different. Douglas,
why do you think eleven years makes a difference?" He
thought for a moment, "Well, I just didn't want to make
her feel strange about being with an older man." She put
her reading glasses on the desk, "How about you? Have
you ever been with an older woman?"

Douglas gave her an honest answer. "No, I haven't." Dr. Martha moved to the chair next to Douglas
as she asked, "Do you find me attractive? I'm not
hitting on you, I'm married." She showed off her very
exotic wedding ring. "I'm just asking. Do you find me
attractive?" Douglas felt a little uncomfortable with the
question but gave another honest answer, "Well, yes I
do." Dr. Martha relaxed a bit and said, "If I wasn't
married and I met you in another situation, do you
think you might like to go out with me? Once again,
I'm not hitting, just asking?"

Douglas was beginning to feel as if someone had
turned on the heat. "We're just pretending, right?" She
smiled, "Yes! I just want your initial reaction to the
question." Douglas took a quick peek at her tanned legs
and trim frame. "Well, based on what I see, you're very
pretty and yes, I would be interested." The doctor
moved back to her desk. "Douglas, I would be interested
in you too; you're a handsome gentleman, and I'm
exactly eleven years older than you." Douglas wondered

how she knew his age. She smiled, "It's on the Bar Association's website. When I saw your name on my call list, I just searched the Internet and there you were." She turned a framed family photo around. "Douglas, my husband is eight years older than me and it's never been an issue. Don't make it one. You're not too old for anything and it's not too late for you to fall in love again." Douglas looked at the photo. "Wow! That was an eye-opener!"

She looked at him. "I want you to tell her how you feel and if she says, well that's nice, but you're too old for me. If she says that, then we talk again. But until that time, I think you should just let things happen." Douglas was beginning to feel much better about his situation. "All right Doctor, I'm going to see her tomorrow evening at a fashion show so, I'll see what happens. Thank you, how much do I owe you?" She stood and extended her hand. "You owe me a phone call on Saturday to tell me what happened. That's all." Douglas shook her super-soft hand, "Thank you, Doctor. I'll call you Saturday."

He left Dr. Martha's office feeling better than he had in a long time. He dropped in to see Billy at the tavern and ordered a gin and tonic. Billy put his drink on a napkin. "Did your friend talk to a therapist?" Douglas raised his glass, "Yes he did and he said it made him feel much better." Billy wiped the bar top as he quipped, "Therapists are just bartenders without the booze!" Douglas finished his drink, "I guess you're right. Good night Billy, I'm turning in early." Douglas walked home; feeling great. As he passed the Doctor's office he muttered, "Thank you Dr. Martha."

Chapter 10

The Fashion Show

Both Marge & Douglas brought a change of clothes to the office. She hung everything in his closet and the work day began. The court dates had been set for two of their clients and Douglas spent the morning working on ways to get each a settlement. He really hated going to court. In the past five years, Douglas had only had to be in actual court, six times. In every other case, he worked out a settlement or appeared at an arbitration hearing. He hoped he could avoid going to court for both of his impending suits. The phones were silent all morning.

Douglas was concerned that he hadn't received any calls. He buzzed Marge. "Yes, Douglas." "Marge, have you noticed we haven't gotten any calls today?" She held up the phone log. "There have been calls but none I had to put thru to you." Douglas wondered why he didn't hear anything. She told him that they had a new phone system. "It's part of the updated computer program. Only line five rings directly to you. That's your private line." Douglas thanked her for the information and asked, "What time are we leaving?"

Marge said, "If we're going in the same car, we're out of here at five." Douglas saluted. "Five PM it is General. Just remind me to get changed." Douglas liked the new system, and he noticed that working without interruptions, made the day pass very quickly. He finally finished the two files and logged off the computer. He hand-carried the files to Marge. "I've finished these, would you look them over and prepare the forms for each?" Marge took the files, "Don't I always look over your work?" He knew she always did. "Do you find mistakes?" She smiled, "Not many, and not often, but some".

Douglas turned toward his office and stopped to say, "Thank you for taking photos at the awards banquet. Next time, tell me so I can suck in my tummy." Marge laughed, "It's nothing that a few visits to the gym can't fix. I'm glad you like the pictures. I know you always forget you have a camera in your phone." Douglas opened his office door. "Yes, I do forget, so remind me to take a few tonight." Marge closed her computer. "I will. I'm heading to lunch now. Need anything?" He told her he wasn't going to eat because they would have food at the fashion show. Marge headed toward the elevator. "I never eat at events like that. The food usually isn't that great!"

Marge left for lunch with some of her office mates. Douglas decided to take a walk around the block instead of eating, just in case there was food tonight, he didn't want to' seem impolite. Outside, the sun was shining and he even saw a bird or two. He found a nice shady spot near his building and sat down as a text message arrived. *"Douglas…don't be late tonight, I've got 2 seats reserved in the front row. See you at 6 - D."* Douglas sent back, *"Looking forward to seeing you and the "surprise" Douglas."*

He opened his media file and retrieved the photo of them dancing in Anaheim. *"That was a really nice time. So, glad Marge hi-jacked my phone,"* he thought. Douglas was still sitting when the ladies of the office returned from lunch. As they passed him he noticed that all but Marge had takeout bags. The ladies waved to Douglas and Marge told them to go on. She crossed the office plaza. "You're out of your cage Douglas. What's up?" He laughed and said, "I just felt like getting outside for a moment."

Marge still couldn't believe it. "Wow, next thing you know you'll be leaving work at five o'clock and going to the gym." He asked why all the secretaries had doggie bags? She explained that those weren't doggie bags. "It's lunch for folks upstairs."

Douglas didn't understand. "You mean the girls bring back lunch for the lawyers?" She said, "Yes, all but me, because my attorney doesn't eat. Don't forget, we're out of here at five today." Douglas took her arm and they headed toward their building. "I got a text from Devin; she's reserved front-row seats for us."

They entered the elevator and headed back to his 7th floor cage! Douglas finished up some work and stopped when the 4:30 PM timer sounded. He picked up his change of clothes and carried a clothes bag to Marge. Douglas entered his small private bathroom and changed into his evening "dress-casual look." He decided not to shave because a little shadow looks good. He was changed and sitting at the small conference table in his office waiting for Marge. She shut down their computer system, picked up her purse and said, "All right, let's get going."

Marge and Douglas headed to the fashion show being held at an Avant Garde loft property in downtown Los Angeles. Once again, his GPS lady got them there perfectly. The valet parking attendant opened the door for Marge and they entered the building which featured stainless steel accents and many sculptures on the distressed concrete floor.

Devin, wearing a beautiful evening resort fashion, spotted them from across the room and waved for them to join her. She hugged Marge and Douglas, and did a twirl. "Thank you for coming." Douglas smiled and told her they wouldn't have missed this event. "Do you like my dress?" Marge touched the fabric and loved it. "It's part of my surprise." She held their arms and guided them to their reserved seats.

"It's great to see both of you." She removed the reserved signs from their chairs, looked at Douglas and whispered, "Take pictures." Douglas put his cell phone in his outer pocket. "I'm ready. Do you have designs in the show?" She smiled and ran her hand along his arm. "You'll find out, just relax. I've got to run, see you after." Marge said, "You look great, by the way!" Douglas added, "Yes, nice outfit, do I know the designer?" She turned and fluffed her skirt. "Yes, you do." Marge looked around at the extremely upscale decorations. "This is very nice, let's get a drink or something."

As if by magic, a waiter, with a tray of drinks appeared followed by a young lady with a tray of snacks. Douglas and Marge took something from each tray and began to relax. The professional decorations including the long beige runway, were lit by several theatrical lighting trusses. There were flowers everywhere. The soft hip hop background music was the perfect choice for the attendees. The waiters continued to service the crowd as more and more of the two-hundred chairs filled.

Douglas noticed that the guests wore a mixture of flamboyant outfits and conservative business attire. Marge commented on the increased level of chatter in the room. There were lots of hugs and kisses all around because everyone seemed to know each other, or pretended they did. An over-dressed man took the chair next to Douglas and extended his hand. "Hi, I'm Eduardo." Douglas shook his hand saying, "I'm Douglas and this is Marge." Eduardo forced a smile, "Pleasure to meet you. Do you design?" Douglas answered, "No, we aren't designers, just guests." Eduardo suddenly seemed uninterested in them as he quipped, "I hope we see a good show."

The music faded for a moment and then dissolved into an up-tempo dance beat. The lights dimmed in the room as the runway lights blasted on, in time with a music accent beat. The next music bump hit and the lights on the new B & B Fashions logo flashed. The announcer said, "Good evening and welcome to B & B's Fashion Preview! Tonight, you'll see a brand-new line of resort wear! There was a music bump as the logo was lit. "From B & B Fashions!"

Douglas smiled because their new logo looked great. The music changed to a semi-loud dance selection which was a perfect tempo for models to time their walks. The first young lady began her turn on the walkway. The announcer described the day/night fashion worn by Victoria. "She's dressed for a day at the beach or just lounging around the pool. This design is by Devin." The model made one adjustment to the ensemble as the announcer continued, "But for early dinner or dancing, with just a slight adjustment, Victoria is ready for that too."

The super-attractive model finished her walk and left the runway wearing the night-time look. The audience loved that first outfit. The show continued with many more resort fashions, each one prettier that the last. Some of the designs Douglas had seen in Devin's portfolio. They showed several very interesting swim fashions for women and men. Both designed to "slim and contour." The announcer wrapped up the event. 'Let's thank all of our models and welcome the new designers! Here's Rocky, Andrea and Devin!" The three designers entered to wild applause and then the stage filled with all the models. Each of the ladies made one final sweep of the stage with the three designers bringing up the rear. Everyone bowed, waved and exited dancing up the runway. The announcer concluded with, "Please join us for our cocktail reception and other announcements about this fashion line. Thank you for being with us!"

The music continued as everyone made their way to the cocktail party. The attendant at the door was telling everyone to follow the arrows upstairs. Douglas and Marge made their way to the second floor while making mental notes of the comments from the guests. Overall, the comments were very positive. Even the over-dressed designer-types were saying they really liked what they saw! Douglas and Marge found the bar and ordered a drink. They saw Devin enter the room. She was being greeted by everyone as she made her way to Douglas and Marge. She hugged them and asked, "Well? What did you think?"

Marge said, "I thought it was beautiful. I really liked the slimming swimwear." Douglas told her it was very impressive. "You're right you had a lot of designs in the show. Was that the big surprise?" Devin shook her head, "No, there's more." Douglas started to say he wanted to talk to her that evening, but he didn't get the words out fast enough because Bernie & Bernice stepped onto the small stage in the corner of the room and called-out to calm the room. Bernie waited and then said, "Thank you all for coming. I hope you liked the show!" The audience broke into rousing applause. Bernice took the microphone. "That's good to hear, because we have an announcement." She handed the mic back to Bernie. "We have posted some of these fashions on our new website." Devin squeezed Douglas' arm.

Bernie continued, "And as a result, we're already getting orders! If any of you want to order anything featured in the show tonight, we'll give you a twenty-five-percent discount." The audience laughed and applauded. He waited for the applause to subside. "But here's the big news, our lawyer and friend Douglas Hedges has put the final touches on the contracts for our new manufacturing center in Florida. We're going to open that facility very soon. Our new full-time designer, Devin Clark is going to run the operation for us. Devin, come up here." She turned to Douglas and whispered, "That's the real surprise."

As Devin moved to the stage Marge noticed a change in Douglas' demeanor. He suddenly seemed very distant. Bernie announced the opening would be in mid-July. "Devin will head to Florida right after the fourth". He handed the microphone to Devin. She looked around the room. "I'm told that we'll be in full production before Thanksgiving. Thank you for coming tonight and I hope you liked what you saw." The audience gave her a nice round of applause. She stepped off the stage and everyone wanted to congratulate her on the promotion. She re-joined Douglas and Marge hugged her. "That's terrific news. I'm so excited for you. You got the job." Devin thanked Marge, "I owe it all to this guy."

She hugged Douglas who said, "All I did was, get you the interview. If they didn't like your work you'd be on unemployment. Congratulations, I couldn't be happier for you." Shelly flew over to them from the bar. She hugged Devin. "It was a wonderful show." Devin was happy her neighbor could make it. The extremely flighty young lady said, "I was late-ish but I have a good excuse. I'm getting married!" Devin didn't know what to say. "That's great news, right?" Douglas asked who she was marrying. Shelly began to ramble very fast. "His name is Justin, he's a studio carpenter. We met on a commercial and we've been going out for about three months. You have to come to the wedding." She looked at Marge, "You come too! Do I know you?" Marge laughed because she had no idea who this jabbering lady was, "I'm Marge, I work with Douglas." Shelly hugged Marge, "I'm Devin's friend and she's going to be my bridesmaid. You will, won't you?"

A totally shocked Devin said, "Sure, I'll be your bridesmaid, but we'll talk about this before the wedding, right? Douglas asked when all this was happening? Shelly continued to rattle on, "Soon! We're looking for a date that we'll both remember. I really have to run. I left Justin in the car, he's just driving around because we couldn't find a parking space. See you." She ran out making a call to tell Justin to pick her up. Devin watched her run out. "Well, that's another surprise for the day. Seems we're full of them."

Douglas felt there were too many surprises for one day for him and didn't want to stay there any longer. He looked at Marge, "You have to get home. And this young designer has to greet her adoring fans." Devin smiled at him, "Which I wouldn't have if it weren't for you." Marge realized that something was wrong but she didn't know what. "Thank you for inviting us, I'll see you at the office, maybe." Devin hugged Marge, "I'm sure. B & B will have some other things they need help with. I hope you liked the surprises Doug. I'll call you when I have a moment and I'll keep you updated." He congratulated her again then he and Marge left the reception area, and bumped into Bernie and Bernice on the way out.

Bernie thanked them for coming. Bernice wondered what Douglas thought about the show. "I liked the whole show, great stuff." Bernie thanked them for hooking them up with Devin, "She's a treasure." Douglas agreed and asked if everything was all set for the Florida property? Bernie told him it was perfect. "We've been looking at buying a condo over there so we have somewhere to stay when we visit the company. I'll send you the paperwork on that." Bernice leaned over to Marge and whispered. "I tried to talk this guy out of sending Devin over there, but he insisted. I hope it'll be okay." Douglas told them that he and Marge had to be running along. Douglas didn't say a word as he walked quickly down the stairs and handed his ticket to the parking attendant. Marge asked, "Is everything okay?"

He quietly said, "Yes, I'm just in a hurry to get going. I've got stuff tonight." Marge smiled, "You've got stuff? Glad to hear it." The trip back to the office parking garage was quiet-ish. Douglas didn't have much to say. He pulled up next to Marge's car and she glared at him. "You wanna tell me what's wrong or do you want me to weasel it out of you?" He said, "Nothing's wrong." Marge wasn't buying his answer. "I've known you long enough to know when something isn't right. Let's see, that girl, ah Shelly is getting married." She looked at him. "Nope, that's not it. Is it something with B & B? Devin moving to Florida? No, that can't be it because, you don't like her. You're right, nothing's wrong. Good night - see you tomorrow."

He looked at his long-time friend. "All right, you got me on this one. Yes, she's moving to Florida and will be busy as the devil. But it's okay Marge, because we never really got involved." Marge sat quietly waiting for the rest of the story. "Sure, I like her, we dance great together and she's grateful that I helped get her a job. But I think that's as far as it goes." Marge laughed, "You run that story by a bartender or two tonight and see if they buy it. I'll see you Monday. Thanks for taking me today. I had fun."

Douglas made sure that Marge got into her car and he followed her down the ramp. She turned right, heading home, and Douglas turned left toward West L.A. Once home Douglas found himself extremely restless. He decided to take a walk to the Village to clear his head and think a little. He continued up the block to the Village Tavern and headed straight for his favorite seat at the end of the bar. As he walked, he called Dr. Martha's service. "Just tell her that Douglas Hedges called. Thank you."

Billy put a napkin on the bar, "Good evening sir. Are you hungry?" Douglas ended the call. "Well, let me have a gin and lemon-line soda first and after a few, I'll let you know about food." Douglas checked his cell phone for messages - nothing new. Billy put his drink on the bar. "It's been quiet in here tonight, let's hope it picks up a bit, I need the tips! Here's your drink, enjoy."

Douglas was reviewing the events of the day and snacking on beer nuts. He couldn't stop munching on them. "I'm a beer nut addict." He found the media file on his phone and clicked on Devin's photo in the red evening dress. He smiled as he looked at the lovely lady. He put his phone on the bar and Billy glanced at the photo. "Douglas, is this your girl?" He replied, "No, she's just an acquaintance." Billy disagreed, "Sorry, but anybody that pretty, can't be just an acquaintance." Douglas reflected on that comment. "That's what somebody else said too. Maybe both of you are right."

Billy picked up his towel and wiped the bar. "If I knew her, I wouldn't be sitting here talking to me! When did you meet her?" Douglas sipped his drink, "About six months ago." Billy asked if they had been out a lot. Douglas grabbed some beer nuts. "No, we haven't. I'm busy all day and she's busy too. She works for a client of mine as a fashion designer." Billy started washing glasses as he offered some bar advice. "If it were me, I wouldn't wait too long." Douglas looked at his drink, "I'm eleven years older than her." Billy looked up after hearing that comment. "That's what's keeping you from asking her out, huh?" Douglas took another sip of his drink. "Yes, why?"

Billy moved to the end of the almost empty bar. "Douglas, my Mother was thirteen years younger than my Dad. They were very happy together. So, I don't think eleven years is too much. But, what do I know? I think your phone is ringing."

"Hello, this is Douglas Hedges. Dr. English, thank you for returning my call." She said, "I thought I told you to call me Saturday, not Friday." Douglas told the very nice doctor that he just saw Devin. She asked where he was right now. "I'm looking at Billy in the tavern. I'm thinking and drinking." She told him to stay there, "I'll be right down."

Douglas told Billy that Dr. Martha was joining him. Douglas finished his gin and ordered another. About three minutes later Dr. English entered and said hi to Billy. He smiled and asked her what she wanted. She pulled Douglas by the arm into a corner booth. "I'll have whatever Douglas is having. He's buying."

Dr. Martha wanted to know what happened. Douglas gave a fast thumbnail sketch of Devin's fashion show and her so-called "good news." Billy dropped off their drinks. Dr. Martha took a taste. "This is very good and different, thank you. Douglas, your trouble really isn't a therapy problem it's just one of judgment. You're not too old for anything so talk to her. Maybe she likes you too, but since you've never shown much interest, she might not tell you."

Douglas looked at the doctor. "Well, my secretary did say that Devin seemed interested in me. She also said the same thing you just said and Billy said that too." Dr. Martha raised her glass. 'See? It's not complicated at all. You didn't really need me. Everybody said the same thing to you." She motioned to Billy for two more. "Just tell her how you feel and wait to see what she says. Either she'll be happy or not. Either she'll say yes or no. What's so hard? I Goggled you and found out you've never lost a case."

Douglas didn't know what that had to do with their conversation. "That's true, I've never lost." The doctor told him to approach this problem like one of his cases. "Put your facts together and win! That's all there is to it." Douglas decided to take everybody's advice. "Okay, I will. The next time we're together, I'll tell her how I feel and see what happens." Dr. Martha smiled, "Good, I'll wait for your call." Douglas asked, "What do I owe you?" She smiled and raised her glass. "A two-drink minimum is fine for now. Call me if you really need me, my hourly rate is less than yours." Their talk was stopped by a car horn. "That's my husband. Goodnight Douglas, Billy." She waved as she left the building.

Douglas settled his tab and headed home. As he walked, he looked at his reflection in a store window and said, "Okay, the next time we're together, I'll tell her and see what happens." Douglas continued walking, feeling better than he did a few hours earlier.

Chapter 11

It's A Grand Old Flag

Marge kept lowering the thermostat in her section of the hallway because the end of June was very hot. Douglas was finding that the new computer system was keeping his billing in check. He didn't have to remember who he talked to, because the computer knew. He was also getting along fine without tons of phone calls every day. He was startled when his private line rang. For a moment, he didn't know what to do as it never rang before.

"Hi, this is Douglas Hedges." It was Devin who laughed and said, "Of course it's you. This is your private number. You're the only person who answers this line." Douglas felt a little stupid but did join her as she laughed at him. "Hello designer lady, what's up?" Marge could see Douglas as he talked on the phone. He was smiling. so she knew who he talking to. Devin was sorry she hadn't called him since the fashion show. "I've been going day and night for the past two weeks. I'm trying to get ready for the move to Florida and had lots of new designs to finish. I want to know what you're doing on the Fourth of July. Please, say you're not doing anything." He checked his desk calendar. "I don't think I'm doing anything, Devin. Why do you ask?"

She wanted to know if he and Marge and maybe her husband could come to a party on the fourth. "I know this is short notice, but I would love for you to come. It's Shelly's engagement party and it should be lots of fun. They've also set the wedding for August twenty-first." He told her to hold on for a moment while he buzzed Marge and asked what she was doing. She had no plans. He told her about the party and she said, "Sure, that sounds like fun." He clicked back to Devin. "Okay. It looks like she can go too. Text me the details."

Douglas asked, "Why is August twenty-first a memorable day?" Devin laughed as she explained, "It's Hawaii statehood day and that's where they want to go on their honeymoon." Douglas smiled, "Whatever works. We'll see you next week. Be sure to text me the details." Devin replied, "I will. The date of the party works out great because I leave for Florida on the sixth. But, I'll be back in L.A. to help Shelly with the wedding in August." Douglas told her he was looking forward to seeing her. "I hope we'll have some time to talk." She assured him they would. "I have a meeting now, so gotta run. Be sure to invite Marge."

Douglas hung up the private line and went into the hallway. "Hey it's much cooler here than in my office." Marge looked at him and smugly said, "That's because I don't have a corner office with giant windows. Close your drapes. Tell me more about the Fourth of July party." He thanked her for the closed curtains idea. "Remember Shelly, that fast-talking girl you met, at the fashion show who's getting married?" Marge nodded. "Well, she's throwing a wedding engagement party on the Fourth and Devin asked if we both could come. She wants you to bring Ralph. They've moved the wedding up to August something and Devin is leaving for Florida on July sixth. I hope you can go." Marge was very excited by the idea. "Oh, I don't want to miss that. It sounds like the social event of the month. Yeah, we'll be there, just tell me where."

Marge called Bernice to tell her about the party. Bernice and Bernie were already invited. "So, let's see if we can't nudge you-know-who along." Bernice agreed and said she was sorry that Bernie decided to send Devin to Florida. The ladies weren't worried, they knew they would fix things.

Douglas received a text message, *"Party @ Elks Club in Buena Park 3 pm (dinner @6) everyone asked to wear Red, White or Blue!!! D."* He told Marge about the text and the wedding target date and their honeymoon destination. Douglas returned to his hot office with a smile on his face. Douglas thought, *"I gotta get a red, white or blue something to wear!"* Marge came in with a memo, "You're gonna love this." She smiled as she read the contents. *"The Lawson Law Group will be closed from tomorrow, July first thru July fifth. We will re-open for business on July sixth. We want you all to have a nice family vacation. Happy Fourth of July! Please inform your clients of the closure. Signed - M. Lawson."* She shrugged her shoulders, "Funny huh? Wonder why?" Douglas turned his chair toward the curtains and then back again. "Because he wants us to have a nice family vacation." Marge turned to leave. "Sure, I've gotta get out of here. It's way too hot even with the curtains closed."

It was warm in Los Angeles. Douglas started keeping his drapes closed which sort-of made him wonder why he had a view at all. *It was party weekend!* He kept thinking, as he strolled thru the West L.A. Village Shops. *"I have to make sure I have time to talk with Devin and see how she feels."* He found a shirt with about twenty American flags displayed on it from Betsy Ross' flag to the current fifty stars. The name of the shirt was "IT'S A GRAND OLD FLAG." That shirt and a pair of jeans would be the perfect outfit.

July fourth opened with a bang! Someone set off a firecracker on the street just outside Douglas' condo. He couldn't believe they were already shooting fireworks! He grabbed a quick breakfast sandwich and coffee, glanced at the TV news and thought he would leave early so he could find the party place. Douglas was a bit anxious, to say the least. He was wondering what Devin would say.

About one-thirty PM, Douglas entered his car, set the GPS and headed to Buena Park. On the way, he began to "practice" what he would say to Devin, and how he would say it. Most of the lines were too corny to be said out loud. He kept thinking, *"I'm a lawyer, I should be able to perform better than this."* The GPS lady said he had reached his destination. He found the Elks Club, but the parking lot was full. Douglas parked about 2 blocks away on a residential street and started walking to the club. It was very hot.

When he arrived, he found a very busy summer carnival taking place. He saw signs that said, "**Bingo in the main auditorium**" - "**Dance class in room 202**" - "**Flower arrangements in room 203**" - "**Cooking demo - kitchen @ 4 pm**" "**S Kline party - second floor**" Douglas assumed that S Kline was Shelly, but knowing her, she could be doing flower arrangements in room 203. He climbed the stairs to the second floor ballroom which was decorated in red, white & blue paper flowers and table settings. The DJ was rocking the room. People were dancing, drinking and having fun. Douglas wondered if this was the right place, was this the right party?

He looked across the room at the various tables and way up in the corner in the front of the room he saw a hand waving. It was Bernie. He made his way thru the mass of people and found a table full of friends and acquaintances. B & B were there, David *(Devin's neighbor)*, Louise *(Shelly's sister)*, Marge and Ralph too. Justin, the groom-to-be came over to meet everyone. Marge asked if Douglas got her text. "The party was moved up to two o'clock. Love the shirt. Very patriotic!" Douglas smiled, "Thank you! I missed the text, I guess. Where's Devin?" Bernie told him that she and Shelly were off working the room. Douglas sat for a moment searching the crowd for Devin, but gave up. "Drinks anybody?" He took a few orders and headed for the bar. As he returned trying not to spill the drinks, he saw Devin across the room.

He motioned with his head for her to come to the table. She smiled and made her way thru the dancers and met up with Douglas. She was excited to see him, "Glad you got here. Did you meet everyone? Nice shirt."

She hoped that everybody was hungry. There's lots of food!" Shelly popped up behind Douglas, put her hands over his eyes and said, "Guess who?" Douglas laughed, "Well, it would have been better if you hadn't talked. Hi Shelly." She released her hands, "Thanks for coming! It's going to be a fun party."

The DJ announced, "Welcome everybody. It's Shelly and Justin's day and we'll hear from them a little later. Right now, I have a surprise for you. I'm not only a DJ, but I'm also a magician. Everyone please turn on your cell phones and raise them in the air." The DJ looked around the room at all the phones being held up. "Great, keep them up for just a moment." The DJ picked up his phone and hit *send*. Moments later every phone in the room dinged. The DJ said, "Look at your phones. What does the text say?" Everyone yelled, "Dinner is served!" The DJ started some nice dinner music as he said, "The line forms on my left."

The dinner music continued as everyone headed for the buffet. Shelly was working the line to say hi to everyone. Devin got her plate and sat next to Douglas. Marge smiled and looked over at Bernice, who was also smiling. Dinner was very nice and everyone talked and relaxed a little after dinner. Justin and Shelly stepped on the stage and took the microphone. "Hello everybody, I'm Justin the groom-to-be, thank you for coming to our party. I want to get things started by having you meet my girlfriend, Shelly. This is an engagement party and my Mom said I'm supposed to ask this. Shelly, Will You Marry Me?" Shelly grabbed the microphone. "Yes, I Will!" The audience applauded and cheered as Justin slipped a ring on her finger and gave her a kiss. Shelly yelled, "Now it's official…We're engaged!" Devin reached over and held Douglas' hand. The DJ said, "Congratulations. Now it's time for the engaged couple to dance; are you ready?"

Shelly & Justin stepped onto the dance floor and assumed a traditional dance position. A sweet sentimental ballad started. They began to sway and then on cue the DJ hit a very hot dance mix. Shelly & Justin broke into a staged, choreographed dance. The happy couple yelled and motioned to both sides of the room. About forty of their friends jumped up and hit the dance floor including Devin who joined Justin & Shelly up front. They had been rehearsing this staged-dance for over a week! The rest of the audience clapped, yelled and whistled as the dance concluded with a jump! The DJ shouted, "Congratulations Shelly & Justin. Now, everybody dance!"

Marge took Ralph's hand. "Let's dance, but not that fast stuff." The music was a smooth foxtrot. Devin joined Douglas. He gave her a small round of applause. "That was great. Now I know what you've been doing." He looked at Bernie, "She's been dancing, not designing." Devin grabbed his hand, "Okay lawyer, let's go." As they walked to the dance floor she said, "Thanks for coming, don't forget the wedding on August twenty-first." Devin and Douglas began to dance to *"The Way You Look Tonight"*

Devin whispered, "The wedding and reception will be here at the Elks on Hawaii Admission Day." Douglas twirled her, "It will be easy to find my way back here. I have it set in my GPS." She looked at her partner and quietly said, "I'm leaving in two days on the sixth, but I'll be back in August. She playfully asked, "Will you miss me?"

Douglas wondered if this was the time to tell her how he felt. He pulled away slightly, looked in her eyes and calmly said, "Yes, I *will* miss you." They continued to dance and Devin began to process the sincerity of his response.

She stopped dancing and looked at Douglas, "I think you really mean that." The song ended, but Douglas didn't let her go. He looked at her and said, "I do." The DJ cross faded into an instrumental version of *"Love's Theme"* as performed by The Love Unlimited Orchestra. Devin held him in dance position. "They're playing our song." She then whispered, "They played this the first time we danced in Anaheim." Douglas smiled as he and Devin continued to dance, holding each other close. As they moved, she began to realize that Douglas wasn't kidding, he really *would* miss her. Devin held him closer as Marge watched from the table.

Suddenly Devin stopped moving. There was a question she had to ask. She whispered in his ear, "Douglas, do you love me?" He didn't answer so she stepped back, smiled and looked in his eyes. "You *do* love me." She moved closer and hugged him tight and kissed him on the cheek. "Why didn't you say something?" Douglas didn't have an answer. He just kept dancing, so Devin took his hand and dragged him to the back patio! A beautiful summer afternoon was about to get better.

Devin looked at her silent partner and without hesitation, kissed him. It was a very long, passionate first kiss. He smiled broadly and held her close as he said, "Yes, I love you and I really *will* miss you. I know I shouldn't feel this way, but I do." Devin pulled away slightly, "Why did you say you shouldn't feel this way?" Douglas took a deep breath, "Because, I'm much older than you."

Devin was having a hard time accepting his statement. "Is that all it is?" He didn't answer. She couldn't believe what he just said. "That's just silly Douglas, because I love you too and age has nothing to do with it." He didn't say a word because he was shocked to hear her say she loved him. Devin hugged and kissed him with more passion than the first kiss. He started to speak but she stopped him. "Douglas, since I was little, I hoped I'd meet a man like you, but I never did." Her dance partner looked a little confused as she took his hands. "I was always trying to find someone who treats women with respect and somebody who's interested in more than just a physical relationship."

She paused and kissed him lightly on the cheek. 'Douglas, I've fallen in love with you because you're an honest, caring person. And in case you're interested, you're not getting away from me." She dragged him back to the dance floor. They danced to *"Loves Theme"* for a moment and then she stopped. "Don't ever tell me I'm too young for you. That's not gonna work! And neither is you're too old for me." They kissed as they danced.

Bernice and Marge watched from the table. Bernice smiled and said, "Isn't that the cutest thing; Devin's in love." Marge raised her wine glass, "Douglas is too." The song ended but Douglas continued to hold his dance partner as he asked, "When is your flight?" She answered, "July sixth at eleven AM". Douglas smiled, "So, we have a little time." As they started toward the table Devin had a crazy idea. "Yes, we do have a little time." She dragged him to the table and looked at everyone, "I have to get ready for my trip to Florida in a few days. I better run! Douglas, can you drive me home?"

It took him a moment, but Douglas took the hint, "Sure, do you need help packing?" She smiled and took his hand, "Yes, I think I do." Devin and Douglas said goodnight to Shelly. She gave the bride-to-be the keys to her VW and quietly asked her to drive the car home.

Douglas and Devin left the party fast. Marge & Bernice clinked their glasses. Bernie and Ralph looked confused. Devin jumped in the car and directed Douglas to the 5 freeway south. The Elks Club in Buena Park was about fifteen freeway minutes away from the hotel where they held the conference.

They valet parked, entered the lobby and went directly to the front desk. Devin asked if room twelve-twelve was available. "We stayed in that room several weeks ago, and it was nice." The desk clerk checked the computer and said, "Yes, it's available."

Douglas put his credit card on the desk, "We'll take it, just for tonight. She has to fly to Florida soon." The desk clerk handed them two key cards as she said, "Have a nice evening." Devin smiled and said, "I'm sure we will." They crossed to the elevator and headed to the twelfth floor. Once inside the beautiful mini-suite, she kissed him on the cheek and put the *Do Not Disturb* sign on the door knob.

Douglas was smiling as he watched his beautiful friend close the door. She hugged him, "Thank you for doing this." He didn't really know what he was doing, but he said, "You're welcome." She took his arm and walked him to the mini-suite's L-shaped couch. Devin removed her shoes, "Wow, I didn't realize how much my feet were hurting." Douglas, being the sharpest lawyer in the room, took the hint and raised her feet to his lap. She smiled, "So, you're a lawyer, a dancer and a foot masseuse?" He smiled back and began to lightly rub her toes. "My dear, I am many things to many people. Just relax, you'll feel better soon." She put her head back against the couch. "Oh, this is good. I would like to order one of these several times a week."

He laughed and continued to caress and massage her feet. "Devin, now that you're in a semi-relaxed state, tell me why you wanted to come here?" She smiled and closed her eyes, "Well, first for a foot rub, then to just get away from the crowd and talk." She stopped and then quickly added, "And have a room service dinner, they have terrific food at this hotel." Douglas told her that he was ready for all three wishes. "Foot rub in progress so, let's talk." She opened her eyes and asked, "When did you fall in love with me?" Douglas paused massaging and started to speak. She said, "Don't stop the massage. I know you can do two things at once." He smiled and continued to gently rub her left foot. "Okay. Here's the truth. The first day I saw you, at the impound lot with your arm in a cast. That's when it started to happen."

She looked at him in disbelief, "Why didn't you ask me out?" He didn't answer. "Ah, the age thing?" He nodded yes. "Did anybody ever tell you that age doesn't matter?" He stopped and said, "Yes, Marge said that a lot." She pointed to her feet. He started again. "But you didn't listen." He moved to her right foot. "No, I heard what she said, but I thought my age would matter to you." She leaned over and kissed him lightly on the lips. "Well, it doesn't. Back to work." Douglas laughed, "You sounded just like Marge when you told me to get back to work."

Devin was in seventh-heaven when her foot rub was completed. "Did you ever work in a salon?" Douglas excused himself and went to the bathroom. "No, but when you get a mani-pedi they always give you a massage. I watch and learn." He returned with a small tube of skin lotion and two small towels. "I'm not finished." He put one towel on his lap and the other on the floor in front of her. "Let me have those feet." She put her legs in his lap, "I really like the service at this establishment, please continue." Douglas rubbed lotion on her feet and then asked, "May I also do your lower legs?" She pulled her skirt up over her knees. "Go for it." He gently applied the scented product on both of her super-soft legs.

"You should go into business doing this." Douglas smiled slyly, "You mean rubbing ladies' feet and legs?" She glared at him, "No, just mine." Douglas put her feet on a towel and went to the closet. He retrieved a pair of slippers. "For you my dear."

She stood and walked toward the large window. "I feel fantastic, thank you." He looked at his lovely friend and asked, "When did you realize that you loved or kind-of liked me?" She turned away from the window.

"The first time we were at this hotel. The way you treated me and held me when we danced, it made me feel special. Marge didn't have to tell me I could trust you, I already knew that." She slowly walked back to the couch. "I just didn't know how or when to tell you and then today, you made it easy." She sat next to him on the couch and kissed him with great emotion. Douglas felt her passion all the way down to his toes and returned her kisses several times. She leaned away from him slightly, "So, what do you think?" He pulled her close, "Devin Clark, I love you, and if you're okay with the age thing, then I'm gonna be smiling every day from now on." He kissed her with even more emotion than the first kiss. She hugged him, smiled and said, "Great talk, let's eat."

Douglas laughed as he walked to the house phone to order dinner for two with a pot of coffee. He didn't notice that Devin had taken a robe from the closet and was changing in the bathroom. He turned around to see the empty room as he said, "Dinner will be along in a few minutes. Where did you go?" He heard a muffled voice say, "I'll be out in a minute. Can you make us a drink?"

Douglas opened the mini-bar and found everything he needed to make them each a very light gin and lemon-lime soda. He put the drinks on the bar and looked up to see Devin in her fluffy white robe exiting the bathroom. She announced, "I'm ready for drinks and dinner." He handed her his gin concoction. They clinked glasses and she tasted the drink. "This is tasty." She kissed him on the cheek and told him there was a second robe in the closet. "Put it on and then tell me about your family and your life." Douglas laughed and did as he was told. Shortly he emerged from the bathroom wearing his fluffy robe and joined her on the couch. "You want to hear about my family? This drink isn't large enough for that story." He did however give her a short version of things which included a peek at his family and his non-stop work schedule. "What about you?"

She sipped her drink and told him briefly about her parents in Connecticut. "That's where I graduated from college. Shelly is about my only friend out here because I've been so busy trying to find a design job." She stopped and raised her glass to him, "Thank you for helping to get my career started." Douglas raised his glass to her, "I just got you the interview. You got the job because they like your designs." Their quiet moment was interrupted by a soft knock on the door. Douglas looked thru the peephole and saw the waiter in the hallway with a cart. He opened the door and the dinner cart was rolled into the suite. He signed for the food, thanked and tipped the waiter.

They continued to talk over their sumptuous dinners. He remembered that Devin loved the stuffed chicken breasts with veggies. It was a big hit again. They continued to talk about the past, the present and a little about the future. For her, it seemed rosy. For him it was the same old thing day after day. She smiled and said, "We'll have to change that. Let's break you out of that mold." Douglas liked the idea but didn't know how his many clients would take it if he changed his spots. She leaned over and kissed him. "Marge and I will work on it for you." He asked if she would like another drink.

She stood and started toward the bathroom, "Maybe later."

Douglas carefully rolled the room service cart into the hall. He opened the lanai door to let in some fresh air and stopped to think about the events of the day. Devin called him from the bathroom, "Douglas, I need your help in here."

He opened the bathroom door to find her in the shower. "Can you to put soap my back." He opened the sliding shower door slightly, pushed up the sleeve of his robe and reached into the shower without looking. She said, "Don't get your robe wet; take it off." He removed the robe and hung it on a hook. He, once again put his hand into the small opening. She poured some shower gel in his hand and said, "Ready?" Douglas didn't know what was going on, so he didn't know if he *was* ready. "I guess I am."

She slid the shower door open, pulled him into the warm water and started laughing. He said, "What's wrong?" She was still laughing when she said, "You're still wearing your boxers." She bent down and pulled his shorts to the floor. "Now you're ready." Douglas stepped out of his underwear and had to laugh as well. She hugged and kissed him as the warm water showered down upon them. "Are you going to put the shower gel on me?"

Douglas was very excited as he began to rub the liquid soap along her back. It had been several years since he had a sexual encounter and never with someone as young and beautiful as Devin. He wondered if he was up to the challenge, but as he touched her super soft skin he realized that he had nothing to worry about. She turned around and applied some of the scented soap to his chest and kissed him. They spent the next moments hugging and swaying back and forth under the multi-head shower. He didn't realize it at the time, but Devin too, hadn't had sex in several years. Even with those obstacles, they seemed to be very compatible. So much so, that the bathroom mirrors got steamy and stayed that way for over an hour. They had a wonderful close encounter.

Chapter 12

Good Morning L.A.

"Good Morning L.A." is what Douglas said as he pulled back the curtains in his corner office. Marge told him it was going to be another hot one today, but he didn't care. His July private festivities had gone beyond his wildest dreams and he was feeling great! Marge entered with today's stack of files. She asked if he was ready to get back to work. He turned his chair away from the city view. "Yes and no. Take a moment and look at the beauty of Los Angeles."

Marge growled, "Yeah, that's very nice, but you have things to do!" He looked at his long-time friend and replied, "You're right, but I've just had the best weekend of my entire life."

Marge knew he had a great time. She listened and tried not to laugh. "I understand, you met a girl and had a fling. I had one of those once on Maui. Met a guy, had three days of wild stuff. He left; I came home and can't even remember his name." Douglas shook his head no, "That never really happened, did it?" Marge just shrugged. He smiled and said, "My weekend was really nice and exciting." She looked at him, "Okay, Mr. Nice. Where is Miss Exciting?" Douglas checked his desk clock. "I think she's about to board a plane to

Florida." Marge started to leave, "Good, then we can get back to work." Douglas picked up one of the files as his private line rang. "Good morning, where are you?" Devin said she was on-board the plane and they just handed her a mimosa.

He smiled, "Sounds like a vacation instead of a business trip." She joked that it was all business, "No pleasure, you know that." He told her he wanted calls and texts all the time." She said, "Yes, I'll have another mimosa and a foot rub please." She couldn't keep from laughing. "Okay there's no foot rub, but I'll be calling. I'll be back soon you know. I have to get fitted for my bridesmaid's dress and attend some wedding rehearsals." Douglas noticed Marge watching him through his glass door. "I know I'll see you soon. Marge sends her best. Bye, Devin." He finished the call and went back to his files, smiling. Marge opened his door a crack, "Must have been a really good weekend." He just looked at her and smiled without saying a word.

The workday continued, Marge went to lunch and Douglas began to wonder if he left early, what he would do. He looked over the morning paper but didn't find much of interest. Putting down the paper, he thought, *"No wonder I work late, there's not much going on."* Douglas called Dr. English and left a message on her service. *"I had a wonderful weekend with Devin. She doesn't think I'm too old for her. Thank You."*

Now it was just a matter of counting the days until Devin returned. Her text messages and calls interrupted him every day but he didn't mind. He kept pressing on because he had to keep his billing hours up. Devin's six weeks in Florida seemed like six months. During her time away, Douglas kept burning the midnight oil and was well on his way to surpassing his billable hours for last month. Douglas noticed that Marge was smiling and laughing on the phone. She buzzed Douglas, "Pick up the phone it's Tony."

Douglas smiled as he answered. "Hi Tony. How are things in Malibu?" He told Douglas it was a beautiful day. "You'd know that if you looked out your corner office window sometime." "That's true, Tony, what's up?" The Chef said he'd been approached to write a cookbook based on his restaurant favorites. Douglas wondered about the deal, "Who asked you about doing the book?" Tony said it was a regular customer who worked for a major publishing house.

"He took some food to his office and they loved the idea. I need your help to understand the contracts." Douglas thought that sounded like an easy job. "I'll drop by tomorrow." Tony said that would be great. "See you then

A Sunday in August

Douglas was watching luggage travel around a baggage carousel at the Los Angeles International Airport. Devin entered the baggage area and quickly found him starring at luggage. She grabbed him from behind. They hugged, kissed and stayed close together as they waited for her bags. He looked at his lovely lady. "You look fantastic." She kissed him on the cheek, "Even after a five-hour flight plus extra time at the airport?"

He hugged her tighter, "Yes, you do. I'll have you home shortly." Douglas found her two matching cases and they headed to her Silver Lake apartment. As soon as Devin closed the front door, she rushed to Douglas and gave him a long, passionate embrace and kiss. Douglas looked around, "It's very quiet here. No beer and cat food?" Devin answered, "Not anymore, Shelly has left the building."

They collapsed on the couch as Devin began to tell him all about the new operation in Florida. She shared some photos on her phone and described the building. She had photos of her new co-workers and she told him what she thought they could do in Florida that they couldn't do in California. It sounded like the operation was going well and that the job was perfect for her.

Devin's noticed that her answering machine was blinking. "Looks like I have a message." She hit play and a very happy-sounding Shelly said, *"Hello stranger. Welcome back to civilization. I'm glad you're here, because I have lots to do this week to pull everything together. I'll call you early tomorrow. Read my note and goodnight."* Devin turned off the machine and said, "Read her note. What note?" Douglas looked around the apartment for a note and found an envelope taped to the refrigerator. "Here's an envelope that says, Shelly's note." He handed it to Devin who started to read it to herself. She stopped and said, "It's from Shelly; let me read it to you.

Devin: I put beer and some pizza in the fridge. Heat it in the microwave and celebrate. I also put new sheets on the bed. If you and that handsome lawyer of yours want to spend the night, you're all set. Just call me early to get me out of bed. Goodnight - Shelly." Devin laughed and looked at Douglas.

"Well, handsome lawyer, are you interested in cold beer, microwave pizza and clean sheets?" He opened the fridge and took out two cold brews. "Let's start with beer and see what happens." He tried for a perfect pour with each glass. Devin looked on and touched glasses with Douglas. "Not bad. Shelly sent me an email about what she needed to do this week. She has lots of things scheduled every day. It reads like hell week only with a better ending!" Douglas said, "If it's going to be a busy week, will I ever get to see you?"

She took a sip of her ice-cold beer, "I *can* squeeze you in a few times because things have changed a little. Shelly spent too much money on the July party and now, they must downsize everything. It's going to be a smaller wedding than planned." Douglas asked, "When you say smaller, what do you mean?" Devin smiled, "Well, there's only one bridesmaid, me. They are getting married at the reception." She finished her glass of beer.

Douglas wondered if there was anything he could do to help. Devin wasn't sure. She yawned. "Sorry it's not you, but it's been a long day for me. I've been up late every night and up real early every morning and I'm still on East Coast time." She kissed him and then kissed him again and then smiled at Douglas. "I could be induced to stay awake and break in the new sheets. Are you interested?" Douglas took the glasses and put them in the sink and motioned for her to follow him to the bedroom.

He kissed her at the doorway, and kept lip contact as he lifted her and carried her to the bed. He put her down gently on the new sheets and continued to kiss her. He also unbuttoned her blouse and began to caress her chest. She whispered in his ear, "One of my models in Florida had to do a fashion show for stripper costumes. She showed me some of her moves. You interested?"

Douglas sat up, wide-awake, applauded and waited for the show. Devin slid off the bed and hummed some stripper-type music. She slithered around removing her blouse and putting it over the head of her one-man audience. She expertly removed her skirt. Douglas realized that his girlfriend had excellent training. He decided to play along and took some dollar bills from his money clip. She turned her back on him putting her backside in front of his face. He took the opportunity to put some dollars in her undies. She undid her bra and slowly exposed her ample breasts. She danced toward her audience on the bed and leaned her naked breasts toward his face. She continued to hum the stripper music as she turned around and began to slide her sexy panties down. That's when she found the money. "Five bucks? That's all?"

"Hey, give me a break. I've never been to a strip club. I don't know how much to tip." She stopped humming and laughed as she hugged him and collapsed on the bed. "Well, I think it's more than five bucks." He rolled over and kissed the semi-nude fashion designer. She kissed him back and told him it was his turn. He looked at her questioning the statement. "Strip!" She began to hum her stripper song again as he reluctantly started to remove his shirt, shoes and pants. She loved the show and pulled him down on the bed so she could hug and kiss him. She said, "I think it's time we break-in these sheets." Douglas kissed her and agreed.

Two hours later Douglas was experiencing a second wind but it was too late. Devin's eyes were closing and she was beginning to snore, ever so lightly. He covered her with a sheet, kissed her on the forehead, set the clock radio for music at six AM and lay down next to his girlfriend.

Chapter 13

I Do Week

Monday

Douglas quickly stopped the music on the clock radio and couldn't believe it was already six o'clock.. He slipped out of bed, kissed his lady on her forehead, and she opened one eye. "Where are you going?" He kissed her again and whispered, "I have to get to the office. Busy day." She closed her eyes and said, "I'll call you later." He smiled, dressed quickly and left her snoozing.

Wedding week started with a frantic phone call from Shelly. Devin was half-awake when she heard her dear friend crying and trying to talk. Devin was having trouble understanding her. "Can you slow down and repeat all of that again?" Devin waited while Shelly began to sob less and after several minutes she blew her nose and started over. "I messed everything up. We can't get married Saturday. I forgot to approve the schedule at the Elks Club, so they canceled our event. I didn't finalize plans with the caterer. I don't have any food or a cake or anybody coming to the wedding." Devin didn't understand. "What? Nobody sent in their RSVP?" Shelly paused and took a deep breath. "No, that's not the reason. It's because I just found the stack of invitations in my purse. I forgot to mail them." She started to cry again. Devin tried to console her long-time friend, but it wasn't working.

Devin offered her an alternative. "Why not get married by a Justice of the Peace at the courthouse? A lot of people do that." Shelly calmed down a little and thought that might work.

"Don't we need witnesses?" Devin told her that she and Douglas would be there. "I can contact the courthouse and get you all set up." Shelly wanted to talk to Justin, "I hope he understands and doesn't get mad. I'll call you back in a few minutes."

Devin called Douglas to give him an update. He found it all hard to believe and then said, "But it's Shelly, so it's one-hundred-percent possible. I'll wait for late breaking news." Devin had another call. It was Shelly again. She said that Justin wasn't that upset and said this way they would save more money. "His family was wondering why they hadn't heard about the event. He's sure they'll come to the courthouse." She wanted to know what she had to do. Devin told her she was looking at the County website, "Just go down to the courthouse and apply for a license. They are open all day. Once you get the license and set the date and time for the wedding, just let me know."

Shelly said she'd get Justin up and moving and get to the courthouse. "I'll call you as soon as it's done." Devin called Douglas on his private line. As usual, he was shocked when the phone rang. She asked, "What time will you be free today? Can you leave early?" Douglas wanted to know what she had in mind. Devin told him that Shelly was going to be busy at the courthouse. "I won't be seeing her today so would you like to take me to dinner?" Douglas told her he had something else in mind. "I'll pick you up at two-thirty."

"Marge, can you cancel whatever I have this afternoon? I'm meeting Devin." Marge joined him with her notepad. "That's easy. You don't have anything scheduled. Where are you going?" Douglas had an evil smile on his face as he said, "I think I'm going to take her to the Italian Grotto."

Marge scrunched up her face, "Remember, you're supposed to be taking me there, but it's nice that you're taking Devin." He smiled and said, "I know. I know. I promised, next time for sure."

They took the long way around and arrived at Tony's restaurant just as the sun was setting over the blue Pacific Ocean. They hugged as they watched the sun sink into the ocean from the parking lot rail. Devin kissed Douglas lightly as they entered the romantic restaurant. The sunset applause had just ended.

Tony saw them enter. "Douglas welcome. Do we have business tonight?" Douglas laughed as he told Tony that this wasn't business. "It's a pleasure trip. You remember Devin Clark?" Tony took her super-soft hand and smiled, "Of course, one does not forget a beautiful woman." She was flattered, "Thank you. But you're making me blush." The owner escorted them to a perfect table and asked if they would like some wine. They said yes as the waiter brought over the menus. Tony quickly snatched the menus and said, "Remember, never a menu for you. You're family." He hurried off to the kitchen as they began to talk about her eventual return to Florida. Douglas raised his glass of wine but didn't take a sip. "Florida is in the future, tonight it's just us. How about a trip to West L.A.? Do you have any other plans this evening?"

Devin told him she had nothing scheduled until she heard from Shelly. "What's in West L.A.?" Douglas smiled and gave her a sneaky smile. "There's a great little bar for a nightcap, which is just a short walk from my condo." Devin kissed the back of his hand, "That sounds perfect." During their candle lit romantic dinner, they talked and held hands from time-to-time. Shelly sent a text with the details about the wedding. It sounded like everything was arranged. Devin sent her a return text. *"Then, relax. Douglas and I will be there."*

Douglas asked if that was a text from her boyfriend. Devin smiled, "No, my boyfriend is busy having dinner with me. It was from Shelly? She says that the wedding was set for Friday afternoon at the court house. We're the witnesses." Douglas wondered about The Elks Club, the dresses, the DJ and the food. She kept eating, "Not gonna happen. I'll explain later."

Tony stopped by to say hello and to chit-chat a little. The owner told Devin that he knew she was the one. "Because Douglas only comes by the restaurant when it has something to do with business." Devin smiled at that comment. "So, I'm the one, huh?" Douglas laughed, "Eat your dinner and don't give me any trouble." Tony hugged each of them and made Douglas promise to bring Devin again. "A beautiful woman always classes up the Grotto." He promised they would return.

The drive to the west side was perfect. They talked and listened to some relaxing music on the radio. Douglas parked in the small lot next to The Village

Tavern and took Devin's arm as he escorted her into the local watering hole. Billy saw him enter, "Good Evening Douglas." They approached the bar, "Billy I would like you to meet Devin Clark a very talented fashion designer." Devin shook hands with Billy, "I guess this guy is a regular around here?" Billy placed a napkin in front of each of them. "Everybody here is a regular. Now you are too."

Douglas held Devin's hand as he said, "Billy how about fixing each of us a special Mai Tai?" Billy went into action, "A special Mai Tai for the lovely lady and one for you, Douglas!"

Douglas and Devin selected a small table and out of the corner of his eye he saw Dr. Martha across the room. Douglas motioned for her to come over. The doctor saw Douglas with a beautiful young lady and quickly joined them. "Good evening Douglas." "Same to you Doctor. Did you just finish work for today?" Dr. Martha said she had a late session, "I'm waiting for my husband."

Douglas tried not to smile too much as he said, "May I introduce Devin Clark. Devin this is Dr. Martha English! She's a psychologist who has an office just down the street." Devin shook her hand, "It's a pleasure to meet you. Won't you join us?" The doctor told them that she didn't want to intrude, "I just wanted to say hello." Douglas asked her to sit for a second. He told Devin that everyone in the village seems to know everyone else. Devin was beginning to get that feeling.

Billy brought the "special" drinks to the table and served them with a flourish. Douglas asked Doctor Martha if she would like a drink. Billy put a third glass on the table. "I brought the Doctor one too." They thanked him and performed a three-way toast. Devin tasted her drink. "This is really good. Everyone here is very friendly." Douglas told her that all shopkeepers know each other and they look out for each other, too. I thought if I ever started a private practice, I would locate here in the village. Dr. Martha asked, "Have you considered that Douglas?" He looked at her and Devin, "Yes, off and on, and then I get my yearly bonus and I say, well?"

Dr. Martha told them, she used to be the same way, "But one day I just said, I'm going solo." Devin asked, "How long have you been a psychologist?" Doctor English thought for a moment, "I got started just before I got married, that was a little over eleven years ago. I've been here in the village for four years." Devin wanted to know what sort of clients she saw. The doctor looked at Douglas and wondered, without saying anything, if this was the girl Douglas was conflicted about. "I see married couples, individuals, everybody, really. I have a very full schedule. What about you?"

As soon as Devin mentioned that she was a fashion designer, the doctor took a sip of her drink and smiled at Douglas. The doctor asked where she worked. "The company has an office here in Los Angeles. I'm also working at their new division in Florida. I'm back here because my friend is getting married on Friday. Douglas and I are going to be their witnesses. Dr. Martha smiled at Douglas, "You're a wedding planner too?" He laughed at the comment, "No, just a witness at the wedding."

Dr. Martha reacted to a car horn. "That's my husband. Great meeting you Devin." She smiled as she looked at Douglas, "Call me next week. I need help setting up my corporation."

He didn't understand. "You don't have one?" She headed for the door, "No, I don't. Not yet. Thanks for the drink." Douglas told her he'd get it started for her on Monday. "Call me at the office." Devin finished her drink and looked at Douglas. "How far away do you live? He took the empty glasses to the bar. "Not far. You ready?" Devin thanked Billy, "Great meeting you." She took Douglas' arm, "Let's go; I'm dying to see the framed email!"

Douglas and Devin hopped in the car, drove around the block and pulled into his secure parking garage. She was shocked at the short drive-time. They took the elevator to the fifth floor and moments later they were in his living room. Devin was smiling as she looked around the ultra-chic top floor unit. She liked the glass doors leading to the open patio with lounges, chairs & umbrellas. Douglas turned on some soft music and his track lighting as Devin found the famous framed email from his ex-wife! "I'm reading it…but I don't believe it! This place is beautiful, why do you ever leave?"

Douglas agreed, but said he couldn't work here. His guest kept looking, "How big is that television?" Douglas wasn't sure, "Sixty-five inches, I think, but I don't get to watch it very often." Devin sat on the couch in front of the TV set. "We'll have to fix that! This is a prime movie viewing location. Wonderful kitchen, popcorn and snacks."

Douglas opened the doors on his bar, "Would you like a drink? I have lots of everything." She asked for something light and watched as Douglas fixed her a "special" light Sambuca with lemon-lime soda and a slice of lime. She tasted his concoction, "This is very good. I like the licorice flavor and it's not too strong. Remember what happens if I have strong drinks." Douglas took her drink and diluted it a little as they moved onto the exterior patio. It was a nice night to relax on the lounge chairs.

Devin stretched out on a lounge chair and looked around the patio area and up at the stars, "All you need is a pool and you're set to go." Douglas pointed up, "My pool is right up the stairs, on the roof. He moved next to her on the lounge and kissed her lightly. She asked if he had neighbors. Douglas touched glasses with her, "No! Not a neighbor in sight." She looked at him, "I've missed you so much." They kissed again and again.

Douglas felt her hands moving down his back. He responded in normal fashion as Devin began to unbutton his shirt, then her blouse. She moved her fingers lightly across his chest then sat up and removed her blouse. She caressed him and kissed him deeply as he unhooked her lacy white bra. She leaned back on the lounge and Douglas began to lightly kiss her shoulders and then her breasts. She realized what they were doing, "Are you sure you don't have any neighbors?" He whispered, "Absolutely." She asked, "But you do have a bedroom, right?" Douglas stopped kissing her chest, "Yes I do. I have two." She sat up, "Show me."

She took his hand as they left the patio area. Douglas locked the glass doors and they moved into the super-size master bedroom. Devon flopped on her back onto the king-size bed and extended her arms as if doing a snow angel. "This is wonderful, I'm not leaving." Douglas leaned down and they kissed as she pulled him on top of her. Douglas glanced over at the clock. It was already ten-thirty. He thought, *"Too bad we started so late!"*

Douglas and Devin were wonderful together. They seemed to know exactly what the other wanted and needed. Neither one had ever had a sexual experience that was so perfect. When the night was over, they both lay naked and exhausted on the bed. Devin whispered, "That was..." Douglas smiled, "Yes, it was. Ready for a shower?" She looked at him, "In a while, I just need a moment to figure out what just happened. It was wonderful." Douglas kissed her, "Yes, it was."

They both just lay on the bed, looking at each other as Devin slowly slipped into sleep mode. Douglas put a light sheet on his lady as he collapsed next to her. It was almost two in the morning, West Coast time.

Chapter 14

Do You Take this Woman?

Friday Afternoon - Courthouse

Douglas was front and center waiting for Devin and Shelly to return from the dressing room. Justin was pacing the hallway as he too, waited for the girls. Marge stepped off the elevator and made a bee-line for Douglas and Justin. "What are you guys doing in the hallway?" Douglas stared at her and said, "We're waiting for Devin and Shelly. What are *you* doing here?" Marge told them that Devin invited her because, "I love weddings."

The guys continued to pace up and down the hallway. Marge laughed at Douglas, "You would think it was your wedding the way you're acting. Sit down and relax." Douglas joined her on the hallway bench, but Justin kept on walking as he waited for his family. He knew they were parking and would be there shortly. It wasn't long until the girls appeared. Marge popped up and hugged the ladies. "Shelly, you look beautiful. Are you ready?" She thanked Marge for coming, "Yes, I'm ready and packed for Maui." Devin joked with her long-time friend, "Wow! You're already packed, I'm very impressed."

A lady with a clipboard stepped into the hallway and asked if Shelly and Justin were there? Justin stopped pacing and Shelly said, "Yes, we are. Is it time?" The clerk smiled and said, "Yes, it is. This way please. Do you have your paperwork?" Douglas handed over the license as the clerk opened the door for the wedding party. Justin's family just made it. They stepped off the elevator and hurried down the hall. The additional six guests made for a full-house.

The ceremony was brief, but much more dignified than Douglas expected. He and Devin did their part and the Judge was very polite. He wished the newlyweds well and asked where they were going on their honeymoon. Shelly was ready for that question, "We're going to Maui tomorrow." The judge told them that Maui was an excellent choice. "That's where my wife and I went on our honeymoon." The wedding party left the courthouse and posed for photos on the front steps. Devin was very happy for her friend and asked, "Shelly, what are your plans for the evening?"

She didn't really have an answer, "Am I really married? It was so fast, I don't have any plans. Did anybody take pictures?" The relatives told her they did. One even had a full video of the service. Shelly was very happy and even happier when Marge told them that Douglas and Devin had something planned for the everyone. Douglas leaned over towards Marge and whispered, "We do?" Marge told the group they had reservations at a beautiful restaurant overlooking the Pacific Ocean. Douglas finally got it. "Yes, we're all going to dinner at The Italian Grotto in Malibu and we have to hurry so we don't miss the sunset." He looked at Marge, "Now I know why you told me to bring my SUV." They gave directions to Justin's family and the wedding party of five piled into the SUV. Marge called shotgun and they headed for the coast. Devin kept smiling as she talked to the new bride and groom.

Marge made a phone call. Douglas asked, "So Marge, when did you set this up?" She raised her hand to him, "Shhh." She called Tony and added six to their dinner party. "See you soon." She ended the call and Douglas again asked, "When did you set up this party?" Marge smiled, "Yesterday, and I added six just now. I thought it was something you and Devin could give them that they would love and would really enjoy." Douglas agreed. "It's a special place. A perfect choice." He told Marge to call her husband and have him meet them there. She laughed and said, "I already did. Ralph loves Italian food and he's probably already there waiting for us." The evening at The Italian Grotto was beyond fantastic. Everyone on the staff went all-out for Douglas and his guests. Marge introduced her husband Ralph to everyone. As the sun began to set, Devin explained the ritual of the restaurant. Douglas smiled and held her hand as everyone sat quietly. The sunset was spectacular and dinner was even better. Marge told Douglas that she already paid for everything. "Or rather, you paid for everything. You know I have your credit card numbers."

Douglas quietly asked, "Did you order a cake too? Marge looked around and hid behind her napkin as she said, "Yes, and a lei greeting for them at the Maui airport, a welcome fruit basket in their room and an island luau all from you and Devin." Tony came by to thank everyone for coming and to congratulate the newlyweds. "Douglas, thank you for bringing Marge. I hope you like my little restaurant." Marge was very happy to be there, "It's beautiful and your food is fantastic." Tony leaned into Marge and whispered, "I want us to have another dinner when these two finally get together." Marge smiled, "I believe they're thinking about it." Douglas said, "I'm sitting right here, you know." Marge didn't care.

Tony placed a manila envelope on the floor next to Douglas' chair. "What's that?" Tony whispered, "It's the recipes for my book. I need you to look them over and if you know someone who likes to cook, I'd like them to make a few of the dishes and tell me if they were easy to understand." Douglas told him that he had three perfect helpers for him. Tony thanked him as he asked, "Is everyone ready for some wedding cake?" He motioned to his staff and they rolled out a very beautiful cake from the kitchen and stopped near Shelly. She was overwhelmed that they *did* have a cake and of course she started to cry. Devin handed her the large knife, "Shelly, you and Justin have to cut the cake." They stood and cut the first piece. The wedding party applauded.

Everyone loved the cake, the Italian coffee and the atmosphere. Since it was getting late, Marge thought they should leave since the bride and groom had to get ready for their big trip to Hawaii. They all thanked the Chef for his hospitality and wonderful food. Tony smiled and said "Thank you all for coming. Marge, it was great to finally meet you. Hope to see you again."

Douglas told everyone about Tony's book. "He wants me to find some people to test his recipes in their home kitchens. Devin said she would try a couple. "When will the book be published?" Douglas didn't know for sure, "I have to review the contracts and he needs feedback on his recipes." Devin thought that Marge would be interested too. Shelly said she would love to make a few things when they returned from their honeymoon.

Shelly and Justin couldn't say thank you enough as Douglas and Devin drove them to their apartment. They were excited to start their new life together and knew that it was already off to a great start. Of course, Shelly and Devin were crying as they hugged and said goodnight. Shelly gave Douglas a tearful thank you kiss. Shelly waved as she watched Douglas and Devin drive away. Douglas handed Devin a tissue. "Looks like you need a box of these." She blotted her eyes and noticed a few tears on Douglas. "I think you could use one too." She dried his cheek as they pulled into his parking structure.

Douglas asked, "Tavern or upstairs?" Devin, using both arms pointed UP, UP, UP. They hugged and lightly kissed as they headed for the elevator. Devin looked into Douglas' eyes and said, "I'll be in L.A. for another week. Will I be able to see you?" Douglas smiled, "Yes, you'll see me, because you're staying here. I'll see you every morning and every night, okay?" Devin kissed him, "Wow! I think I'm gonna like it here." They got on the elevator and as the doors closed, Devin kissed him again.

Chapter 15

Time Passes Slowly

Justin and Shelly returned from Maui sunburned, tired and happy. They had sent photos from the beach that Devin framed and placed on her design table in Florida. She broke the news to Douglas that she wouldn't be able to leave for Los Angeles until Thanksgiving Eve. Douglas took the news in-stride and just kept working non-stop trying to keep his mind on business. He and Devin attempted to talk on the phone several times a week, but with the time difference and work schedule, it wasn't easy.

Marge knew they were having trouble connecting. She thought of a possible solution, "You have a client in Florida, why don't you go visit?" Douglas knew that wasn't possible, "That's a good idea, but I've got too many plates spinning here. Devin will be back soon." Marge, the queen of sarcasm said, "She will, unless she meets someone in the Sunshine State." He laughed and countered with, "That's not nice!" Marge touched her telephone ear piece. "Law Offices…One moment, please. You have a call from your mom on line one."

Douglas picked up the phone. "Hi Mom, how you folks doing?" She told him they were fine. "Will you be coming over for Thanksgiving?" Douglas said he was thinking about it, "Can I bring a guest?" His mom excitedly asked, "Is it a girl?" Douglas cautiously said, "Yes, it's a girl. Why do you sound so surprised?" She replied, "I didn't know you were seeing anyone. We look forward to meeting her. We'll see you in November."

Douglas wrapped up the call with his mom and got back to work. He made a note to mention Thanksgiving to Devin. The days passed. Some quickly, some dragged by. From time-to-time Douglas would glance at his award on the wall and drift back to the very nice weekend he had in Anaheim, which seemed like a lifetime ago.

On October fourteenth, Marge entered the office carrying a cupcake with one lighted candle. Douglas looked up, "What's this?" Marge smiled, "It's our anniversary, thirteen years working together." Douglas stood to accept the cupcake. "Wow, that's longer than some marriages." Marge laughed, "Longer than yours, for sure." Douglas agreed, "Well, thanks for the cupcake. I owe you a present." Marge blew out the one candle, "If you insist." He looked at her and felt he had to say, "Marge, I would've been lost without your help all these years."

She was really smiling at that comment. "Yes, you would. You don't even understand how the intercom works. On that present thing, just give me your credit card and I'll go shopping." He opened his wallet, "All right, I know you won't break the bank. Get yourself something nice." He handed over his credit card. Marge thanked him and said she'd be gentle with the card. "When does Devin return to L.A.?" Douglas explained that she had to attend a design convention and wouldn't be back in town until just before Thanksgiving. Marge asked what he was doing for Turkey Day. Douglas told her about spending the day with his family.

Marge said, "Good. That's better than last year. Remember, you weren't here." Douglas thought for a second, "That's right, I was in Boston. I had the Turkey Dinner Special at Denny's. This will be a lot better. Mom's a great cook." Marge needed more information, "So, Devin will be in town?" Douglas was trying to avoid the question, "Yes, she might be. Why?" Marge kept asking questions, "If she is, will you take her to meet your family?"

He didn't know. "I haven't mentioned it to her. She might not be interested." Marge smiled, "Well, if you take her, I expect full details." He promised he'd give her a full report. "Can I get back to work now?"

During the next phone conversation with Devin, Thanksgiving with his family was mentioned. She loved the idea and said "Yes, if you agree to meet my Mom and Dad too." Before Douglas could answer she asked, "How about, going to Connecticut for Christmas?" He wasn't ready with an answer for that so he said he'd check his schedule and let her know. They talked for almost thirty-minutes and Douglas kept looking at Marge who was trying to get him to get back to work by holding up a file.

He ended the conversation as Marge entered his office. "This is important and needs to be dealt with fast." He took the one-inch file and put it on top of the stack on his desk. He asked her to find out when the office would be closed over the holidays.

About two hours later she had the complete schedule which she copied for Douglas. He read that the office would be closed from the twenty-fourth of November thru the following Monday the twenty-eighth. She reminded him that usually very little got done around the office on the Wednesday before Thanksgiving, because of the company lunch, "So, leave early and you'll have a nice quickie vacation." Douglas asked Marge, "Do you have the Christmas schedule also?"

Marge didn't have it yet, but asked, "Are you doing a family thing at Thanksgiving *and* Christmas?" He told her what Devin had in mind. "Looks like I might be going to Connecticut to meet her parents at Christmas." Marge loved that news. "Oh, this is big! This is 'shout it from the rooftops' big." He glared at her, "Marge, not a peep about this." "Sure. I was only kidding. I just wanna be a fly on the wall for both family events." Douglas told her he'd take photos and give her a full report.

Marge had an idea for him. "I know what I'm going to suggest goes against you winning another award next year, but what if we told all of your clients that we'll be closed from Christmas Eve until the first week in January." He didn't think that was possible, but he'd consider it. He said, "I think it'll be fun to visit Connecticut at Christmas. I'm hoping it's going to be cold and look like a scene from the movie Holiday Inn." He wrote the dates on his calendar with question marks and would make sure to mention everything to Devin. He looked out the window, then at the stack of files on his desk. He took a deep breath and spied his gift plaque. He quoted the statement, "GET A LIFE" and wondered *when or if* that would ever happen.

Chapter 16

Light or Dark Meat?

Devin was back in L.A. with a nice tan and a holiday twinkle in her eyes. She arrived on the overnight flight, the red-eye as it's called. The plane encountered a weather delay and arrived very late. By the time the flight landed, it was early Thanksgiving morning. She hugged and kissed Douglas while they waited for her bag. With all the hugs, he missed her suitcase several times as it passed on the luggage carousel. On the way to his car Devin asked if they could eat something before going wherever they were going. It was early and Douglas didn't think there would be much traffic, "Sure, we have time."

Douglas smiled to himself as they pulled into the only 24-hour restaurant they saw, Denny's. She wondered what was so funny. Douglas hugged her and explained where he ate last year on this day. "Seems that history repeats itself." They both laughed and ordered Pumpkin pancakes and coffee. He looked at his beautiful overnight traveler, "I'm glad you're back." She leaned over and kissed him on the cheek, "I'm glad I'm back too, I missed you." He hoped she wasn't too tired to meet the family. She said she was ready for them. "I hope they're ready for me."

They didn't rush breakfast. They sat, had coffee and talked about Florida and the future. When they finally hit the road, they encountered a freeway full of holiday traffic. Devin had a few more details about the Florida operation but she dozed off in the middle of a sentence. Douglas smiled and pushed her head back and continued to grin all the way to his parents' place. He had to slow down several times for accidents and crept along through a two-mile long construction zone. It also seemed that every car in Los Angeles was heading south which meant the trip took over twice as long as normal. He awakened his passenger almost four hours later as they approached the three-story San Diego home. It was a windy, but beautiful Thanksgiving Day. She checked her hair and makeup in the sun visor mirror. He looked over and smiled and told her, "You look great!"

They rang the bell and Douglas yelled, "Hello, we're here, and we're hungry." Mom and Dad were waiting by the door. "Devin, these are my parents." Mom cut him off, "I'm Sonya and this is William, welcome to our home." His brother Michael and a young lady wearing an apron entered the hallway from the kitchen. "Happy T-Day bro, and who is this lovely lady?" Douglas smiled, "This is Devin Clark and the ugly guy in the hallway is my little brother Michael." Michael smiled at Devin and introduced his girlfriend Angel and said, "I'm glad you both came. Doug is kind of hard to get to know, but we can tell you all of his secrets."

Everyone but Douglas laughed as they entered the family room. Devin looked around and said, "Very nice to meet all of you. You have a lovely home Mrs. Hedges." The lady of the house said, "We're Sonya and William Hedgegroves, not Hedges." Devin was confused and turned to Douglas, "You changed your name?" Douglas quietly said, "I've been meaning to mention that, but…" Sonya looked at Devin and explained. "Mr. Lawyer here decided that Hedges was easier to remember. So, he changed his name, but we love him anyway."

Devin laughed and grabbed Douglas by the shoulders. "So, you're not who I thought you were. What other secrets do you have?" Michael told her not to go there, "It's a black hole of secrets." Douglas shook his head and wondered if coming here was a such good idea. "No, it isn't a black hole." Sonya told Devin that Douglas had been a very good student. Michael yelled from the kitchen, "Yeah, we all know that Mom, top of his class, dean's list, etc., etc."

It was time for dad to come to his son's rescue. "Mother, give it a rest. Does anybody want a drink?" Douglas answered, "Sure Dad, make us something." He whispered to Devin that his dad loved to make drinks. Sonya said, "He used to be a bartender in his other life." Douglas tried to change the subject by telling Devin that Michael was a television studio carpenter. Brother Mike said he'd been very busy lately. "I'm working with a commercial company and the work's been steady for over a year. The company just got several big clients so, I guess I'm gonna stay busy."

Sonya walked around and stood between her two boys. She put her hands on their shoulders. "This is nice! Both of my sons are doing well. Now if they'd just get married, I'd be really happy."

Douglas said, "That's always the theme around here." Devin tried to add something to the mix, "I've been working in Florida. My assistant is getting married next month." Sonya sat next to Devin. "Florida huh? Doing what?" Devin explained that she was a fashion designer currently working for one of Douglas' clients. Douglas joined them from the bar. "She's very talented, Mom. She's going to have her own fashion line someday." Mom wanted to know how long she'd known Douglas.

Devin knew that question would come up. "We met in January." Sonya looked at her and said, "And?" Devin didn't know what to say, "And? Well, we're very compatible. We have a good time together. We both taught ballroom dancing and I missed him like crazy when I was in Florida." Sonya told Devin that her oldest was a good man, "He just hasn't been too lucky with the ladies." Douglas, once again, questioned his decision to join the family for dinner. Dad jumped in again, "Please don't start the old girlfriend stories, Mother." Sonya didn't know why not. "Devin should know about his past."

Michael and Angel wanted to get in on this tell-all session so they joined the group in the family room. Devin looked at everyone and said, "Yes, tell me all about his sordid past." Douglas knew he was about to be embarrassed because his mom and brother were going to do their version of a "tell-all" book about little Douglas Hedgegroves. They talked about his first girlfriend, that torrid affair that lasted less than two weeks, the no-dates for the Junior or Senior Proms, his ex-wife and the email message. Douglas got red and redder if that was possible.

Mom realized that they were torturing her son so she turned the conversation to Devin. She asked about her career, the new job and her plans for the future. Devin did a wonderful job explaining everything. It all sounded great to the family.

Sonya announced to the room that Devin seemed like the perfect girl for Douglas. "Do you have any wedding plans? Douglas was now, totally mortified. "Mom, please."

Sonya continued, "Well, I'm just asking because you're slow. You're a lawyer! You need facts. Facts - schmacks!" She moved behind William and put her arms around his neck. "I knew your father for about four months and that's all the time I needed." William reached up and touched her hand. "I knew she was right for me. How many years ago was that?" Sonya smacked his shoulder, "Too many! But you get the point. You should know by now."

Devin looked at Douglas and said, "I *do* know." She opened her handbag and removed a light-blue ring box. She handed the box to Douglas who looked confused. "Douglas Hedges, I mean Hedgegroves, I love you! Will you marry me?"

Douglas slowly opened the blue box and removed the ring. He stopped and looked at everyone in the room who appeared to be shocked. They were waiting for him to do something. He realized the seriousness of the moment and looked at Devin as he said, "I love you too. Yes, I'll marry you." He slipped the ring on Devin's finger and she kissed him. The family yelled and hugged each of them. Dad said, "Oh, this calls for something special." He started placing glasses on the bar top.

Sonya was still busy hugging everybody. "Really? Did that really just happen?" She glared at Douglas, "Did you know about this?" She looked at both of them, "Did you guys have this planned?" Douglas told everyone that he didn't know anything about it. But he was glad it happened. He took Devin in his arms and kissed her again as they received congratulations from everyone. Dad broke out the bubbly and everybody toasted the new couple.

Sonya raised her glass. "Congratulations, you two. We sure have a lot to be thankful for today." She asked about Devin's family. Devin told her that she and Douglas were going to visit them for Christmas in Connecticut. "We'll announce our engagement over there at that time." Douglas laughed, "Okay, I'll practice being surprised. What?? Me?" Sonya looked at Michael. "So now, just one more to marry off." Michael looked at his brother, "Doug why did you have to do this here?" Douglas shrugged his shoulders, "I didn't know about it! It really was a surprise. Wait till my secretary Marge hears about this." Devin hugged her guy. "Marge already knows. She was in on the planning." Devin handed her cell phone to Douglas. "She's on the phone"

"Hi Marge, thanks for the great surprise. It was really unexpected." She told him he needed a little prodding, "I hope you like the ring." He looked over at Devin and held her hand. "Yes, I love the ring and the lady who's wearing it." Douglas asked, "How did you pull it off? Marge told him it was easy. "I talked to Devin and told her to go pick out a ring. She did, and I gave the jewelry store your credit card number. Remember when I used your card to buy my anniversary gift?" Douglas smiled. "Yeah, I remember." Marge laughed, "Well, it was a very expensive gift." Douglas laughed hard with her. "Thank you Marge, now stop crying. She wants to talk to you." He handed the phone to Devin. The ladies talked and cried together. Douglas shouted, "Happy Thanksgiving Marge."

Sonya and Angel had the table ready and dinner was served. Everyone said a short prayer, and then William asked the standard T-Day question, "Light or Dark Meat?" Following dinner everybody got to learn a little more about Devin. She used their small laptop to show some of her designs. They all liked the work and hoped she would be able to move back to L.A. soon. There were other suggestions too. Maybe Douglas would take the Florida bar exam and move over there. Michael brought out the "family photos" and Devin got to see "chicken legs." That's what they called Douglas growing up. He was scrawny, to say the least.

Mom was crying as Douglas and Devin left! Michael sent them off with big hugs. Everyone had a great day. Douglas couldn't stop smiling on the ride back to L.A. Devin asked, "Did you really like the surprise, chicken legs?" Douglas couldn't wipe the smile from his face. "You know I did, and please don't call me that. I'm glad you and Marge cooked it up." She asked, "Do you think you can do it all over again at Christmas?" He glanced at her and said, "It will be my finest performance. You didn't drink too much wine, tonight did you?" She smiled and said, "No." "How about Turkey? Too much turkey can make you sleepy." She showed her ring and said, "No! I didn't have much of that either."

The newly-engaged couple celebrated for over an hour in the quiet of the West L.A. condo! Devin finally nodded off still wearing her ring! It had been a very long day! Douglas glanced over at her as she slept in his extra-large bed. The ring was a perfect choice, it looked great. He kept thinking, "*how he could be so lucky!*" He knew there was a lot to consider, there were so many possibilities for the future. It was an exciting and unforgettable Thanksgiving Day and night. Douglas thought to himself, "*This was a lot better than last year at Denny's, for sure.*" Douglas kissed his future wife on the forehead as he thought, "*Doctor English was right I guess it's never too late for love.*"

Chapter 17

It's the Holiday Season

The office was festooned with small Christmas trees and garlands. Douglas knew that his workload would slow-down soon; it always did at the end of the year. Marge was busy overseeing the annual holiday party, making sure everyone got a Secret Santa note and trying to fit actual work into her days. She asked Douglas if he wanted any holiday decorations for his office. His answer was simple, "No. That way there's nothing to clean up in January." She had another question as she was leaving, "Have you talked to Devin lately?" He told her that he called her almost every evening. "She said her family was very excited that they were going to Connecticut for Christmas."

Marge announced that Douglas had a call on line one. It was Bernie who had a new manufacturing contract that needed to be finalized quickly. Some businesses in Los Angeles were slowing down, but the fashion game had deadlines that had to be met. They talked for over an hour and decided that after Christmas, Douglas should hop over to Florida for a few days to look over the operation, meet with the manufacturing company and iron out the new contract additions.

Douglas and Marge worked on his December and January schedule. He needed to get to Devin's parents, then to Florida and then back to L.A. and still keep his clients happy. Marge contacted the travel agency in the main lobby and within the hour, they gave her the perfect itinerary. She entered the office with a fax from Bernie and told Douglas all about his holiday plans. "You'll fly to the East Coast and arrive late in the evening, two days before Christmas. You'll return to L.A. just after New Year's. It's all done." With that out of the way, he went back to work on Bernie's fax.

Marge popped back into his office to ask when he was going to tell everyone that he was engaged. He looked up, "How about when I return from Florida? Then it will really be official, since both families will know." Marge liked his thinking on the announcement. "You know I'm dying to spread the word, but for now, shhh! I get it." She handed him his Secret Santa card. "What's this?" She told him to read it. *"Your Secret Santa gift goes to William Christopher."* He put the card in his briefcase and went back to work.

That evening, while walking to The Village Tavern, he saw a silver business card holder in the window of a quaint knick-knack shop. He entered and after feeling the weight, decided that it would make a nice Secret Santa gift. Douglas crossed the tree-lined street brightly lit with thousands of holiday lights. Each store looked festive and inviting. He entered the Village Tavern which was decorated way more than normal. Billy, wearing a Santa hat waved, "Good evening Douglas, haven't seen you in a while."

He took his favorite stool at the end of the bar, "I've been busy. Lots going on." He looked around and complimented Billy on the holiday décor; "It looks very Christmassy." His cell phone interrupted their conversation. He saw Devin's name on the caller-ID. "Holiday hugs my dear." She wanted to know if he had his travel plans. He told her to check her email. "I sent you my full schedule. I'll be with you for Christmas and all the way through New Year's too." Billy overheard his conversation. "You won't be here for New Year's Eve?" Devin heard him in the background. "Who's that?" Douglas laughed, "That was Billy. I'm at the Tavern. Can I put you on speaker?"

She said, "Sure. Billy, I'm sorry but Douglas won't be with you on New Year's Eve, because he's going to be right here with his fiancée." Billy yelled, "Fiancée! Congratulations, drinks are on me tonight." Douglas laughed, "Too bad you're not here Devin; Billy is buying me a drink! I should get engaged more often." She laughed back and said, "Not gonna happen Mr. H!" He took Devin off-speaker and asked her to run the plans by her family to make sure everything was okay. Douglas wondered about accommodations at the family home because some folks are a little uneasy when they have house guests. Devin assured him that it would be perfectly alright for him to stay at their home. She said, "They have plenty of room and in Florida, no problem, you're staying right here with me. I'll clean off the sofa for you." They said goodnight, as Douglas turned to his free drink. Billy dried his hands and applauded Douglas, "Congratulations! When's the wedding?"

Douglas didn't have a clue. "We're both super busy but we'll work it into our schedules." Billy wanted to know how he popped the question. Douglas milked his free drink and told Billy about Thanksgiving at his parents' place, and Devin's big surprise. Billy thought that made the holiday even more special as he raised his glass of club soda. They toasted and Billy said, "Here's to a life of surprises."

The days leading up to Christmas were full of distractions. Marge had all the Secret Santa gifts collected. She liked the weight of the gift Douglas brought and put it under the company's holiday tree with all the other presents. Everything would be handed out tomorrow, the twenty-first at the holiday party.

Douglas came in early on party day because he knew they would be knocking off at lunch and he had several things he had to finish up. Marge arrived a bit early too, for real work and then party work. This would be the last day Douglas would be in the office this year. He wanted to make sure he had everything wrapped up and then he could leave with a clear head. He also left a nicely-wrapped package on his desk with a big tag.

TO: MARGE

Do Not Open until CHRISTMAS!!!

Douglas attended the office party and received a very nice-looking leather cell-phone holder from his Secret Santa, Mrs. Wells. He wished her and everyone Happy Holidays as he headed out. "Merry Christmas to all. See you next year." He pushed the down button and said to Marge, "I think there's a box with your name on it on my desk. Merry Christmas! The elevator doors closed. Douglas loaded his stuff in the car and headed to West L.A. He still had some packing to do because he just remembered that it was cold back there.

The airport shuttle arrived before dawn and Douglas was on-time for the early flight to Hartford. The first-class section wasn't full today. The flight attendant brought him a cup of coffee and the breakfast menu. He was about to turn off his cell phone when he received a call from Devin who asked, "Hi sweetheart, where are you?" He said, "Good morning, my dear. I'm on the plane, it's pointing east and I should be at the White Plains Airport at six o'clock tonight." She told him that was about an hour away from the family home. "I'll see you there."

Douglas, a lifelong California guy, was chilled to the bone when he stepped into the windy twenty-eight-degree night. Devin pulled up in a snazzy SUV and tooted the horn. She opened the rear hatch and he quickly put in his bag and slid into the nice, warm car. Devin looked great wearing cold-weather clothes. He gave her a quick kiss but his lips were so cold he almost didn't feel it. She told him they expected more snow tomorrow. "It's gonna be fun." She asked if he'd ever been sledding. He hadn't. "I used to see snow on the mountains from my office window, but that's as close as I ever got to the white stuff."

They pulled into the driveway of Devin's family home; a very beautiful double-story colonial style made from weathered brick, with a red door and white shutters. The place looked great in the glow of the holiday lights which adorned the porch. Devin couldn't resist. She scooped up some snow from the front yard and made a baseball size snowball. When Douglas closed the rear hatch, she got him! "Welcome to Connecticut!" Douglas shook off the snow as they entered the house which resembled a fairytale castle. He looked around at the glowing fireplace, the holiday lights and decorations, and of course, the gigantic Christmas tree in the living room bay window. *This really is a movie set*, Douglas thought.

Devin's parents, Charles and Mary Clark were overjoyed to see their daughter with "her Douglas," as mom called him. They told the attorney to dump his stuff in the hallway and join them by the fire. Charles asked if he would like some holiday punch. Devin said, "I'll get some for him Dad, what about you?" Charles told her that he and Mother would both have one. "It's an occasion for sure." Douglas looked at her parents, "Yes, it is." Douglas couldn't help but notice how much Devin resembled her mother. They could almost pass for sisters. Mr. Clark wanted to know what time he left Los Angeles. Douglas looked at his watch. "I left the house before the sun was up, I had a layover, I guess about eight or nine hours total. I rested a little on the flight." Mary said, "So, this will be your nightcap. It's hard flying from west to east." Charles raised his glass, "You'll have it better going back."

Devin told the family about their plans following Christmas, "We're going to fly to Florida and Douglas will get a chance to see our offices down there and meet with our manufacturing wing." Charles thought that was a good idea, "You're the one that set the Florida operation up for them, right?" Douglas finished his drink, "Yes, for B & B fashions. They have been my clients for many years." Mary smiled, "And that's how you met Devin." Douglas looked at the young lady sitting next to him and nodded, "Yes, it is."

Charles picked up the empty drink glasses, "Douglas, we want to take you on a tour of our little town tomorrow okay?" Douglas smiled at Devin, "That would be great. I want to see where you grew up." Devin dragged him to his feet, "That's tomorrow. Now, it's bedtime mister lawyer."

Douglas, aka Mr. Lawyer smiled and grabbed his bag and followed Devin upstairs to the first door on the right. It was a quaint room with a small single bed and lot of pink all around. Douglas was very tired and just plopped his coat down on a waiting chair. *"I'll unpack tomorrow,"* he thought, as he sat on the very soft bed. She leaned over and kissed him lightly, "I'll see you in the morning." He waved as she closed the door and then slouched back against the pillow. When he opened his eyes, it was already light outside.

He noticed that his bag and clothes were in the closet and his toiletries were neatly arranged in the bathroom. It seemed that a not-so-little elf named Devin had come in quietly, put his stuff away *and* charged his phone. She also put out a nice sweater for him to wear. *"This has to be the work of my girl,"* he thought, as he showered, shaved and dressed. When he went downstairs to the family room just off the kitchen, everyone was already there having coffee. He smiled at everyone, "Good morning, what time is it?" Charles raised his coffee cup. "It's seven. You're just in time for breakfast."

Devin entered the dining area with a pot of coffee, "Good morning sleepyhead." She filled his cup. Douglas looked at his lovely lady, "Thank you for unpacking me." She moved to her dad's cup. "You're welcome. I put your batman undies in the drawer." Douglas laughed but her dad didn't understand that comment. Devin just smiled at Douglas and said, "Can I interest you in some eggs? He was sort-of distracted by the view out the bay window as he said, "Sure. Is that a river?"

Mrs. Clark entered from the kitchen saying, "Yes, that's why we love this place. You always hear the water and lots of birds too." Douglas asked if Devin was raised here. Devin put her hands on his shoulders. "Yes. You slept in my old pink bedroom last night."

Christmas Eve was off to a nice start. During the morning, they gave Douglas the grand tour of their little town. It reminded him of the Village where he bought his condo. They showed him the ivy-covered college and the theatre where Devin used to work. The tour was short because Charles and Mary were hosting their annual Christmas Eve party at their home. This year was a special occasion because they wanted their friends to meet Devin's guest. Douglas wanted to know when his big acting debut would be. Devin told him, "Tomorrow, when we open our presents." Douglas remembered, "I don't have any presents for anybody." Devin hugged him and whispered, "Yes you do, you put them under the tree, remember?" Douglas smiled and finally got it, "Yes, I forgot, it's been a long week."

The Clark's holiday party was very nice and unlike Los Angeles affairs, it started early in the afternoon, on-time, and ended early too! Devin clung to his side as Douglas was introduced to what seemed like everybody in town. Of course, he didn't remember many of their names and that's where she came to his rescue. They remembered his name and joked with him about being in the cold for Christmas. Many hoped it wasn't too cold for a California guy.

Charles and Mary turned in about ten PM leaving Douglas and Devin sitting quietly by the fire. The glow from the Christmas tree also lighted the room. Douglas looked at Devin and kissed her. "I'm here with you, but I still miss you." She thought that was sweet and kissed him again.

Douglas told her he liked her little town but didn't think he could survive here. "As we drove around today, I looked at a lot of signs. Is there anything open past nine PM?" Devin put her head on his shoulder, "Not much, that's one reason I left." He kissed her on the nose. "You look beautiful in your cold-weather clothes." Since they were old, she was glad they still fit. Douglas got serious for a moment. "Have you given any thought to what we're going to do?"

Devin looked around to make sure they were alone. "You mean about getting married and beyond?" He hugged her, "Yes. That's what I mean." She smiled and snuggled into his chest, "Well, no and no! Have you?"

Douglas looked at the beautifully decorated tree as he said, "Yes, I have. We get married by an Elvis preacher in Las Vegas and broadcast the wedding "live" on your website so everybody can see it." She knew that wasn't the real answer, "Let's just set a date, and then fill in the details."

Douglas told her, "It has to be based on your schedule. I'm stuck in L.A. My routine is always the same." Devin said she would speak with B & B and come up with a date. They kissed again and put their sock-clad feet on the coffee table. He decided to ask a semi-serious question, "How many guys have stayed in your old room before? Devin sat up slowly and looked at him, "None! This is a very straight-laced society around here. They frown on that sort-of behavior." He kept asking questions, a technique he learned from Marge, "Didn't you have dates in high school?" She didn't want to answer, but did. "A few, but they never got any further than the front door." Douglas gave her an evil glance, "Ms. Clark, are you telling me that I'm the first man you ever brought home to meet the family?" She was embarrassed, but she answered quietly, "Yes." Douglas was looking for the right words, "And you left high-school a virgin?" She nodded yes without saying a word. "That's really something."

He knew he had to lighten-up the conversation. "Well, guess what young lady? You're not having sex tonight, either. Not until we get to Florida, because I'm respecting your parents' lifestyle. Is that okay with you?" Devin leaned over and kissed him. "That's very sweet. And you wonder why I love you! Douglas, you're wonderful."

She hugged him, "I was worried about you coming here. I didn't know what you would think about my parents and this town." Douglas assured her that he thought her parents were terrific and he really loved the town. "I could never live here, but I can see why they love it." She kissed him again and Douglas wanted to break the mood again so he quipped, "I can't believe you never messed around in high school." Devin looked at him and said, "Nobody really wanted to get to know me. I was the geekiest girl, super tall, with a bad complexion who sat around all day drawing. I didn't fit in. Even in college I was an outsider." She looked around to make sure they were alone and whispered, "Are you ready for the full Devin story?" Douglas dropped the smile and nodded yes.

She got very quiet, "I didn't want to attend school here. I wanted to go to the big city. I went to college in California and I met a guy who seemed very nice. We went out a few times and I thought he really liked me. Then I found out that he was seeing two other girls at the same time and making jokes about the tall girl he had to go up on." Douglas was about to smile, but he stopped. "I confronted him about it…and…he hit me. I tried to fight back but, couldn't." She began to cry softly as she talked, "He really hurt me Doug, he kicked me and then tried to rape me, but that wasn't gonna happen! I picked up a vase and smashed him in the head. He really bled a lot and took off yelling, "I'll get you for this." Douglas said, "I hope you reported the attack."

Devin took a breath and continued, "Yes, I called the campus police, but they didn't do much. I talked with the local police too, but nothing happened. I spent the next week looking over my shoulder every place I went. Then I saw him. He had a big bandage on his forehead that covered his left eye. He saw me across the quad and started yelling that he was gonna get me for doing this to him."

Douglas put his arm around her shoulder, "I'm sorry to hear that. What finally happened?" She looked at him and realized that he wasn't judging her. He really cared. That made her very happy. "Well, I went to the Dean and told him I was leaving school because of these events. He tried to talk me out of it, and when he said he hoped there wouldn't be any trouble or repercussions from this incident, I got mad! He didn't care about me. He just didn't want any trouble, so I left school the next day and came back here.

Douglas hugged her and asked, "What did your parents say about everything?" She just looked away and didn't answer. "You didn't tell them, did you?" She leaned against his shoulder, "You're right. I never mentioned it. I've never discussed it with anybody, except you. It's our secret, okay?" He kissed her on the forehead, "Of course it is." Devin seemed to be relieved. She moved to the fireplace and poked the logs to make the fire come back to life and straightened the hanging Santa stockings as she talked.

"I told Mom & Dad that I missed being here and wanted to see my friends. I had my college credits transferred and received my degree at the local college." She moved to the couch and sat on the arm. "That's why I haven't dated much or had many boyfriends. I've always been afraid." She looked down at Douglas, "When I met you, you were nice to me. I couldn't believe that you were helping me and that you didn't expect … sex in exchange."

Douglas pulled on her hand and she slid down the arm of the couch and landed next to him. "That's quite a bit for me to digest. You're all right now?" She kissed him on the cheek. "Yes, I'm fine, now." She paused and said, "There's a little more to my story, but I think you need a drink first." She took him by the hand, led him to the kitchen. He sat on the comfortable bar stool, watched her open a beer and split it into two glasses. Douglas took a sip and said, "I'm ready for part two."

She held up her glass, "Well, since this is my tell-all day, here's the rest. You're only the second guy I've ever been with. The first was in college, here. Since then, I've just been too busy to get involved and didn't really want to. Douglas took a sip of beer. "That's hard to believe since you're so beautiful. But, if you say it's so, I believe you." She hugged him, "It is!"

Douglas told her that he was married only that one time for two years, and it seemed right. He put his hands on her cheeks. "But, I didn't feel about her the way I feel about you. He kissed his lovely fiancée'. Devin smiled and asked, "How did you feel when she left?"

Douglas smiled, "I think I need more beer for that conversation." Devin opened a second bottle and split it with him. "Thank you, fiancée'. Now that I think about it, when she left, I really didn't feel much. I've always wondered how her daughter Elizabeth felt. She was only seven at the time. Did she care about leaving me? I was hurt because I thought they both loved me, but I guess they really didn't. You do! I know you love me, right?"

It was Devin's turn to lighten the moment, "Yes, I love you for about a billion-reasons!" She grabbed his hand and dragged him back to the living room fire. He said, "I want to hear all of them." She plopped next to him on the couch. "Here goes. You think about me and what's best for me. I've told you before, when we're out you never look at other women. You're always looking at me."

Douglas raised his right hand and with a smile he said, "Okay, I promise from here on, I will not ignore all those other girls when we're out. I'll start looking around." Devin hit him with a throw pillow. "Just, try it!"

He smiled at her, "Devin, I don't want to look at other ladies." He put his arm around her shoulder. "I just want to be with you. I've never had a lasting relationship like my parents or yours. I think we could have that. That's how much I love you." They kissed again, this time longer and more sensual. She pushed him back on the couch and kissed him tenderly. Douglas squirmed and said, "We better knock this off and get to bed because Christmas will start early, I'll bet. She agreed, "Yes, we better go because one of us is getting very excited and since Santa will be here soon, we don't want to shock him." Douglas laughed, "I think both of us are getting excited. Merry Christmas Mrs. Hedges."

Devin took his hand and guided him toward the stairs. "Merry Christmas, Mr. Hedgegroves. You're right, that's hard to say and remember. Let's make it Hedges or Clark." They kissed goodnight and headed slowly upstairs to their separate rooms.

Chapter 18

Christmas & Beyond

Christmas Day began with Douglas watching the light snowfall through the bay window in the kitchen. Devin served him a toasted English muffin and coffee and explained that they always have their *real* breakfast after they open presents. She and Douglas sat holding hands in the quiet of the morning and he asked if they could step into the backyard for a moment. She didn't know why, but she led the way. The half-engaged couple stood in the chilly morning air listening to the babbling stream and catching a few snowflakes on their faces and hair. Douglas was smiling as he hugged his wife-to-be. "This is my first snowfall, you know. It's so peaceful and quiet." She kissed him on the cheek and whispered, "I'm glad you're here." Then she quietly said, "Don't move." She put her hand on his cheek and slowly turned his head toward the water.

Douglas couldn't believe his eyes. A young deer was camly walking across their property. The fawn stopped, looked toward them standing together in the yard and silently walked away leaving only tracks in the snow. Devin asked, "How did you like the floorshow?" He looked for words to describe the moment but only said, "I loved it. That was amazing." The intensity of the snowfall increased and Devin suggested they head inside, "It's time to open presents."

They dusted off the snow and joined her mom and dad in the living room. Devin told her parents about the deer and her lawyer's reaction to his first snowfall. They were glad he got to experience all of that. Mom started the festivities by handing Douglas a nicely-wrapped present as she said, "We're so happy you could join us. Merry Christmas Douglas." He smiled and waited as he didn't know their Christmas traditions. He looked at Devin who said, "Well, open it. I want to see what Santa brought you." Douglas started to open the wrapping neatly but Devin jumped in and tore the paper off the box. "That's how we do it around here.' Douglas opened the gift box and loved what he saw; a beautiful silk Aloha Shirt with a note that said, *"Something to wear when you're not being a lawyer - Santa."* Douglas showed the gift and note to Devin. She loved it too. "You can wear that in Florida."

Douglas watched as Devin opened a cute little present from her mom and dad. She smiled when she looked at her new wrist watch. "Thank you. How did you know that mine didn't work anymore?" Mom told her they noticed she wasn't wearing her favorite watch in any of the photos she sent them from Florida. "We thought it was something you could use." The family exchanged a few more packages, tore off the wrapping and put it on the pile. Devin crumbled some of the paper and threw several balls at Douglas. He tossed one back and it landed in the fireplace. Mr. Clark said, "You beat me Douglas, that's what we do with all the paper." They opened everything under the tree except three small envelopes. Devin motioned to Douglas to do his thing. He leaned down under the tree and handed out his three gifts. He was dying to see what *he* bought the family. They each received gift cards to local stores. Mom said, "Douglas how did you know these are our favorite places to shop? Thank you."

Douglas said, "A little bird told me," as he pointed to Devin. His intended looked at him and raised her eyebrows and mimed the words, *"You ready?"* He nodded yes because he knew it was time for act two of the proposal show, and he was well-rehearsed. Devin said she had a special present for Douglas. Her parents looked as she stood holding a small package and of course, Douglas acting as if he had no idea what was going on.

She remembered the speech she used at Thanksgiving almost word-for-word and handed him the blue ring box asking, "Douglas Hedges, will you marry me?" Douglas smiled, looked at the ring and turned in an acceptable *(Three out of Four stars)* performance as he said, "Yes, I'll marry you."

Mr. & Mrs. Clark were very happy with their show but Mom said, "We already thought something like this was on Devin's mind since she had never brought anybody home to meet the parents." They asked when they would have wedding plans. Douglas was still pretending to be shocked so, he didn't have an answer. Devin told them it was too early to set a date, "But once we figure that out, you'll be our first call." During their lovely late Christmas breakfast and holiday dinner Devin kept flashing her ring. Douglas watched and smiled as he replayed the story Devin shared with him last night in his mind. He was happy she never mentioned any of those events to her mom and dad. *"There's no reason they ever have to know,"* he thought as he looked across the table. It was a wonderful day with Devin's family and just a hint of snow.

The shuttle picked them up the following morning for their early flight to Florida. Devin's parents were tearful as they waved goodbye. On the way to the airport, Douglas checked in with Marge; there were no problems. He told her the ring surprise show went well and that he had photos of everything.

The flight south was on-time and nice. They slept most of the way and stepped off the plane into the warm Florida sunshine. Douglas seemed to come alive in this temperature, a lot more than in the cold. The cab dropped them at the industrial-looking B & B office building. Inside, you could tell it was Devin's workplace because there were lots of designs stuck on the walls. She scooped up a small pile of mail near the door and said, "Let's head up to my place." They stepped in the elevator, she inserted her key and hit PH. The ride only took about twenty-five-seconds. They stepped off into Devin's large, almost unfurnished, loft on the top floor of the building.

Devin explained, she didn't need much furniture because she was always downstairs working. Douglas set his bag on the floor and called Marge again, not thinking about the time difference. "Sorry Marge. I forgot we're in Florida. We're fine and officially engaged." She wanted to talk to Devin. He passed the phone and the "girl-talk" went on and on. When asked, Devin said, "Yes, he did another award-winning performance of the proposal scene." Douglas listened and listened and the humid weather caused him to doze off in a very comfortable lounge chair. She woke him in-time for dinner and some late-night engaged couple fun.

The next morning, Douglas wearing his Christmas Aloha Shirt, met with the manufacturing company and got the new contracts signed in record time. They wanted a few changes, which were easy to make and everybody left the meeting happy. Devin got to see her boyfriend in action for the first time and was very impressed, "You are a very good lawyer. I'm glad you're taking care of this." Because of Douglas, B & B would get their new products made for a much lower price starting next week. He called Bernie and gave him the good news. B & B were very grateful.

Devin took Douglas on several sightseeing outings and to the beach. They had fun in the warm Florida sun, did a little shopping and Devin made them a quick dinner. "Whatever you're making smells wonderful." She held up a recipe card, "It's Tony's Special Spaghetti Sauce." When their early dinner was over, they sat on the balcony and watched fireworks for a while. Later in the evening, they heard a group of partying people in a nearby apartment counting down to the New Year.

Devin, looking fantastic in her super tight short skirt, danced over to Douglas and kissed him, and then kissed him again! She said, "Happy New Year Mr. Hedges." He hugged and kissed her, "Happy New Year soon-to-be Mrs. Hedges." She thought they should just bring in next year without leaving her place. Douglas liked that idea. She unbuttoned her blouse and asked two questions. "When are we going to bed? And, when

are we getting married?" Douglas pulled her down.
"Bed now! Married, sometime this year. Happy New
Year!" They kissed and welcomed in the holiday for
over two hours. It was a lot better than watching the
Times Square Ball Drop. They decided that when
Devin went back to L.A. in several weeks, that's when
they would tell everyone about their engagement.

The next morning, Douglas called her from the
boarding area. "Yes, last night was the best New Year's
Eve I ever had." He had to cut the call short because it
was time to board the plane. He smiled all the way back
to LAX. Once the wheels hit the tarmac, Douglas turned
on his phone and called Devin. He left a message on her
voice mail and then called Marge who told him about his
schedule for tomorrow. Douglas told her, "I'll be there
with bells on." Marge laughed and told him to just be on
time. "No need for bells, Happy New Year!"

Douglas grabbed a cab at LAX and headed to his
West L.A. Condo. He called Devin again and left
another message. The following morning was the first
work day of the year. Douglas broke with tradition for
the first time in many years, he didn't look at the email
from his former wife. He just headed to work and when
he entered his office it felt like he hadn't been away.
The place was busy and Marge wanted to tell the world
about his engagement. He promised she could tell
everybody when Devin was there. Douglas was
counting the days.

In the late morning Devin finally called. Her phone
had been shut off while charging. She said she talked to
B & B and they arranged for her to fly back to Los
Angeles on the thirteenth. Marge put the date on the

calendar and then looking over her notes from last year, she started smiling as she entered the office. Marge asked if he knew the significance of the thirteenth of January.

Douglas had no answer. Miss know-it-all told him, "Last January thirteenth, you went to the impound lot and met a certain young lady for the first time." Douglas was shocked, "That was a year ago?" Marge nodded, "Yes it was, so you better do something really special when she gets here." He assured Marge that he would, as he went back to work.

During the next ten days, he worked long hours, late into the night for several new clients. He even slept on his office couch a time or two because he was just too tired to drive home. Lately, he'd been keeping fresh clothes in his office closet, so nobody was the wiser, except Marge. Douglas bought a very cute one-year gift for Devin, and decided to take her to Malibu for dinner.

January 13 - 4:30 PM

Douglas was waiting once again by the baggage carousel as he checked the arrival times. Her flight had landed. Marge called and needed some information on a client file. Douglas was trying to explain to her where to find what she needed when two soft, perfumed hands covered his eyes. Douglas said, "Marge either Devin is here, or I'm being man-handled by a beautiful model. Let's talk later." A sultry voice asked, "Guess who?"

Douglas smiled as he turned around, "It's a wonderful fashion designer?" He kissed and hugged her. She hugged him back. "Yes, that's what I am all right." Douglas attempted to retrieve her bag which was a little difficult because she was clinging to his side. When he finally snagged the bag he said, "I think you missed me." She hugged him tighter. "And you didn't miss me?" He kissed her on the cheek, "Yes, I did." She grinned at him, "I know you did. Marge told me." Douglas pushed her toward the car. "Let's get going! I have a plan." She entered the car, "Marge said you had a surprise for me. Douglas smiled, "I have no secrets anymore." She patted his hand, "That's okay, I love surprises."

They exited LAX and headed toward the ocean. Devin talked about their new designs and how the manufacturing that he helped set up was working out great. She was dying to tell Shelly about the ring. They turned North on Pacific Coast Highway.

It's was a beautiful day for this drive. Devin was very happy. "I think I like the Pacific Ocean better than the Atlantic. It's closer to you." She looked around at the surroundings, "I know where we're going." Douglas smiled as he looked at his passenger, "But, I'll bet you can't guess why." She thought for a moment, "Because we're hungry?" Douglas told her that was one reason. "Because you want to tell me you love me in a beautiful setting?" He said, "That's true too, but the real reason is that today is our one-year anniversary." She was shocked, "You mean it's been a full year since I met you?"

Douglas parked the car at the Italian Grotto. "That's right soon-to-be Mrs. Hedges; one year ago today I met you and your beat-up yellow VW bug." He grabbed a small gift bag from the back seat. As they walked toward the door Devin said, "Time really flies, doesn't it? I can't believe everything that's happened since that day."

Douglas agreed, "Yes, and here we are again, Happy Anniversary."

Tony saw Douglas enter and kiss his lovely guest. He joined them, "Good evening Douglas. I see you've brought this beautiful lady back again." Douglas proudly said, "Tony, she's not just a beautiful lady; she's my fiancée." Devin showed the ring. Tony hugged her and then Douglas, "I knew the first time I saw you that you'd be together. Congratulations!" Tony escorted them to their "special table". Douglas told Tony that this was also their anniversary, "I met her one year ago today." Tony hugged Devin, "Happy Anniversary. Sit, have some wine and relax."

Tony moved quickly towards the waiters and told them about the engagement. They brought glasses, wine and water. Soon an appetizer arrived—mouth-watering Bruschetta. Douglas put a small bag on the table. His darling lady asked, "What's this?" Douglas told her he couldn't allow their first anniversary to pass without giving her a gift. She held up the small bag, "Douglas you embarrass me, I don't have anything for you." He touched her ring finger, "Yes, you do, you're going to be my wife. There, I said it." She rustled through the tissue paper and found the gift, a great-looking scale model of a yellow VW Bug painted exactly like her car. She noticed that the left front headlight was busted.

Devin started to tear-up as she looked at Douglas, "You are the sweetest man I ever proposed to." She leaned across the table and kissed him quickly. Douglas pulled out his phone and snapped a photo of Devin holding her gift. He then asked the waiter to grab a shot of them as they posed with the VW. Douglas saw Tony smiling at them and they asked him to get into a photo with them. The waiter snapped a group shot and Devin took the camera. She wanted to see the pictures.

She scrolled thru the three photos and then saw one or two he took at the recent fashion show and several Marge took of them dancing at the company party. Douglas was enjoying the ocean view and wasn't watching Devin with his phone. She kept looking and found the original photo of her car, with the broken left-front headlight. She looked at Douglas and showed him the picture. "You really did just bump my car. You only broke the front headlight." Douglas laughed at her, "I told you that's what I did." She put down the phone, "But you said you didn't have a photo, when you did. This shot proves you just broke the light. You didn't have to pay for anything."

Douglas took a sip of his wine, "Well, I guess I didn't have to pay, but remember there was a problem with the photo file. I just felt it was the right thing to do, and look what I got out of it. I got a wife." She leaned over and kissed him, "And look what I got, a wonderful man."

Tony approached, "I hate to interrupt the love making, but it's time to eat." Devin hugged their host. "Tony, you are the sweetest man." He laughed, "I agree, eat, enjoy and save room for your dessert. It's being made for you right now." Devin told him she'd been making recipes from his cards. Tony paused and asked, "Did you like them?" She told him they were wonderful. He smiled and walked away with a little more zip in his step than normal. "We owe that guy a lot, what can we do for him?" Douglas laughed, "Name our first child

Tony. Devin laughed as she said, "Our first, how many do you want?" Douglas laughed, "Let's talk about that later; right now, let's eat!"

The Vegetable Lasagna was wonderful; the "special dessert," his Luscious Hot Fudge Cake, was outstandingly special. Douglas handed Tony his packet of recipes with notations from Devin, Shelly and Marge. "The recipes are great. How's the book coming?" Tony replied, "Everything is on-track. Thank you for fixing the publishing deal." Devin told Tony, "I fixed many of your dishes for my co-workers in Florida, and everybody loved them." They hugged and thanked Tony and the staff for the terrific dinner and dessert. As Douglas and Devin headed back to the condo, they talked about the future and what they wanted out of life. The more they talked the more they realized that they both wanted the exact same things.

Douglas turned off the living room lights, closed the bedroom door, and looked at Devin with her pillows propped against the headboard. She said, "What? What are you looking at?" "I'm looking at the most beautiful woman in this room, with the softest skin I ever felt, and the greatest legs I've ever seen; and I'm thinking to myself, I'm the luckiest guy in this condo." He tossed his cell phone on the bed, "I know you're dying to call Shelly so, let's tell her."

Devin dialed the number, Justin answered. They talked for a moment and then Shelly took the phone and the girls started to yack. Douglas headed for his well-stocked bar and heard Devin say, "I'm in West L.A. at the condo and we have news. We're engaged!" Shelly screamed so loud, Douglas could hear her all the way in the kitchen. Shelly wanted the details. Devin filled her in on everything while Douglas made them each a Mai Tai with little umbrellas. Douglas kept motioning that it was bedtime and finally, Devin gave in and ended the conversation.

Douglas turned off his phone and set it to charge. "It sounded like Shelly was happy for us. Now, we have to do the same thing with Marge and everyone at my office and all the B & B staff here and in Florida." Devin loved the idea, "Yes, that's our project for the next few days." She raised her glass, "Happy Anniversary, Darling."

They kissed as Douglas dimmed the lights. It had been several weeks since these new lovers had seen each other. They celebrated their anniversary for a very passionate two-plus hours. It was the end of another wonderful day!

Chapter 19

Time to Tell the World

Monday, January 16th

Douglas attempted to get showered and dressed for the office quietly so he wouldn't wake his sleeping beauty, but it didn't work. She heard him floundering around in the semi-dark bedroom and asked, "Where are you going? It's not even light outside, is it?" He leaned over and kissed Devin on the forehead. "I have to get to the office early to get some work out of the way because you're coming to meet everybody and that means Marge will be distracted." She reached up and used his tie to pull him down for a nice good morning kiss. He told her to take her time and grab a cab to the office. "Just let me know when you'll be arriving." She smiled, put the pillow over her head and said, "Okay, hubby-to-be. I'll see you in a few hours or so."

Douglas had been working on several new client accounts for over two hours when Marge arrived at her desk. "Well, look at you, Mr. Early Bird." He told her that Devin would be there a little later. "You can drag her all over the office and tell everybody about our engagement." Marge was very happy. "You know I've been dying to do this since Thanksgiving! Do you know how hard it's been for me to keep my mouth shut?"

She returned to her desk, smiling and then turned back to Douglas. "You did say, yes didn't you?" Douglas nodded his head, "Of course I did and I know how hard it's been for you. Thanks again for helping with the ring. It really was a big surprise."

Marge came back and hugged him, "Not as big a surprise as my Christmas present. Ralph & I want to thank you for your generosity." Douglas was a little embarrassed, "Well, you did say I couldn't do this job without you, and when I thought about it, I realized you were right. I felt I had to share my bonus with you. I hope you and Ralph can use it." Marge smiled, "We sure can. Thank you, Douglas."

Devin arrived at the office just before ten, and Sergeant Marge took over. She escorted her down the hall to meet Mr. Lawson, then every associate and their assistants. Even the janitorial and lobby staff met Devin and saw the ring. While all of that was going on, Douglas called Dr. English and was prepared to leave a message when the Doctor answered.

"I'm shocked that I actually got you on the phone. I wanted to give you some news; Devin and I are engaged. She proposed to me over the holidays. She likes surprises, you know." Dr. Martha loved the good news, "I told you, age was not an issue. She really does seem like the perfect match for you." Douglas thanked her for prodding him and told her that the paperwork was returned for her new corporation. "I'll drop it off at your office later today." The doctor said, "Anytime will be fine. If I'm not here, just slide it under the door. What do I owe you? Douglas smiled as he said, "Two beers! Okay?"

He ended the phone call just as Mr. Lawson entered his office. He wanted to congratulate his top attorney on his engagement. "I want you to know that it's alright if this puts a crimp in your billable hours. You'll make it up later. She's a lovely lady and I wish you all the best." About eleven-thirty, Marge and Devin finished making the rounds and they landed back in Douglas' office. Marge hugged the wife-to-be, "I know you won't remember anybody's name, but they will remember yours, the soon-to-be, Mrs. Devin Hedges!"

Devin thanked Marge for her help and collapsed on the office couch. "Now, we have to tell B & B. Can we take them to lunch?" Douglas loved that idea. "Let's meet them at the beef-dip sandwich place near their office." Marge said she knew that restaurant, "Let's say one o'clock." Douglas said he'd finish up quickly and told Marge to come too. Devin loved the view from the corner office window. "Can you see the ocean from here?" Douglas looked up, "Only on the one clear day a year."

Lunch was set. Marge and the happy couple went to meet Bernie & Bernice at their favorite beef-dip restaurant which was just across the street from their garment-district offices. B & B were seated in a back booth and were smiling when they saw Marge, Devin and Douglas. They hugged and then Devin told them the good news. B & B said they knew it all the time, "Ever since you first danced together." They loved the ring and the story about the double engagement shows. Devin told them, "I picked it out and Marge paid for it with Douglas' credit card she just happened to have in her purse." Bernice laughed and said she loved that story.

During their beef-dip lunch, they *did* talk a little business. Bernie thanked Douglas for stopping off in Florida to get the new manufacturing going. Bernie said, "I think we might have a problem coming up. We'll know later today!" Bernice said now she understood why Douglas was so willing to spend a few extra days in Florida. She hugged Devin, "It wasn't because of the fashion business; it was because of this *other* business." Marge enjoyed the lunch but knew that she and Douglas had to get back to the seventh floor hot-box. Devin hugged her guy and asked him to pick her up at B & B's later.

That evening, Douglas learned that Devin had to return to Florida tomorrow. There was a problem with the new manufacturing company. B & B got her a seat on the first flight in the morning. The shuttle would pick her up at four-thirty AM at the condo. They pulled into their parking garage and Devin asked what they were doing for dinner. "I'm taking you to Montrose. It's a quaint Village restaurant with great food and wine."

Devin loved the quiet candlelight ambiance of this local establishment. It was much more elegant that she expected. "I feel like I should be wearing a ball gown. This is beautiful and it's just moments from our place." Douglas smiled because she said, "our place." During their romantic dinner, he asked if she knew when she would be able to move back to Los Angeles. She reached over and took his hand. "Hopefully by July. B & B want me to be their regional representative. I would oversee their expanded operation here on the West Coast and the new offices in Honolulu, which haven't been set up yet." Douglas loved the idea of having her based here in Los Angeles.

After dinner, they made two stops. He slid a large envelope under Dr. Martha's door and they dropped by The Village Tavern to show Billy her ring. It was getting late and Devin knew she had to pack for her early flight to Florida. They had one quick drink and off they went toward the condo. During their leisurely stroll, they stopped several times to hug and kiss under the stars. Devin put her head on his shoulder as they walked, "You are really spoiling me, I could get used to this. Sorry, we didn't have much time together this trip, but soon we'll be together so much, you'll be sick of me."

Douglas opened the door of his condo and asked, "Should we live here after the wedding?" Devin stretched out on the couch, "I love this place since I'm the first woman to be here." She sat up quickly and looked at Douglas, "I am the first, right?" Douglas laughed and said, "No, you're actually the twenty-seventh."

She flung a small couch pillow at him. He ducked and said, "You know I'm full of beans. Of course, you're the first." She looked up at him from the couch. "I know, and that's why it feels like my real home." Douglas told her it was getting late, "You have to get up early, let's go." He leaned down and she thought he was going to kiss her but instead he scooped her off the couch and carried her to the bedroom. Devin loved the gesture but told him, "Please, put me down. I don't want you to break anything." The night was ending and another separation was about to take place. Douglas moved in next to Devin on the bed and held her in his arms, gently kissing her forehead, until she fell asleep. It was another perfect ending to a wonderful day!

Three AM came around about eight hours too early. Douglas didn't sleep much that night. He just lay in bed holding his fiancée. His eyelids closed from time-to-time but, for the most part, he was wide-awake and loving every minute of it. Devin opened her eyes and hugged the love of her life. "Is it time to go?" Douglas told her the van would be there in an hour. "So, get in the bathroom. I put your carry-on by the front door."

She was moving at a snail's pace because she really didn't want to go. Douglas helped her out and hugged her as they waited in front of the building. The shuttle was always a little early. They hugged again and she promised to call him as soon as she arrived and then every day, twice. The driver loaded her bag which gave the lovebirds another chance to say goodbye. She kissed him, "I gotta go. I'll call you. Love you!" Douglas kissed her back and said, "Love you, too."

The shuttle departed and Douglas felt a sense of loneliness as he slowly made his way back to the condo where he dressed and then dragged himself to an early breakfast in the very busy small café on the tenth floor of his office building. He looked over the menu on the board in the hallway. The selections sounded good, so he ordered at the counter and took a seat. On the other side of the room he saw Marge reading the morning newspaper. He waved and she dropped the paper and joined him. "Good morning Douglas. Have you been here before?" He said, "No. I always forget the place is here." She wanted to know why he was there so early

He explained that he was up very early because Devin had to take the morning flight to Florida. "They are having manufacturing problems and I have tons of work that I was supposed to do yesterday, but we had lunch out of the office and I had to leave early." They had a nice chatty breakfast. Marge didn't know Devin was leaving and she tried to pry wedding details out of him, but there weren't any. She offered a few suggestions of chapels and themes and added a few honeymoon suggestions too. Douglas just listened, ate his breakfast sandwich, drank his coffee and didn't say a word. As soon as they got to the seventh floor, they were besieged with client calls and things that needed immediate attention. Seems the New Year was the time for problems to pop up. Douglas continued non-stop until way after lunch. Marge buzzed him and he looked up. "There's a call from a Mary Clark on line one."

Douglas wasn't sure that he knew a Mary Clark, but took the call. "Hello, this is Douglas Hedges." The woman on the phone explained that she was Devin's mother. Douglas smiled and asked his future mother-in-law what she needed. Mary asked if he'd heard from Devin today. Douglas checked his watch. It was after three o'clock. "No Mary, I haven't." Devin's mom said she knew her daughter was flying back to Florida early and should have arrived by now. "She never called us."

Douglas asked for Mary's number. "There might be something wrong with her phone. I'll check on it, and call you back." Douglas went into the lobby and explained to Marge about the phone call and what was going on. "Devin said she'd call when she landed. Can you check the airline to see if the plane landed on time? Ask B & B for the flight details since they made the reservation."

He called Devin's cell, got her voice mail and left a message to call him ASAP. He then called the Florida office, to find that nobody had seen her yet. They said they would have her call as soon as she arrived. Marge entered his office without a smile on her face, "That flight landed over four hours ago and she wasn't on the plane."

Douglas was confused, "She wasn't on the plane? Marge, call the shuttle company we always use and see if her van was on time. Maybe they were late and she had to take a different flight." Douglas checked his email and there was nothing from Devin. He looked up and saw Marge on the phone. She seemed very upset as she entered his office again and closed the door. "Douglas, the shuttle company said that her van was involved in a major accident on the 405 freeway. It must have been bad. They said their driver and one passenger were killed. The injured passengers were taken to the California Medical Center."

Douglas grabbed his keys and headed for the door as his cell phone rang. He looked at the caller I.D. It was Devin! "Devin, where are you?" A male voice said, "Is this Douglas?" He didn't move, "Yes, I'm Douglas Hedges." "Mr. Hedges, I'm Sgt. Pollack of the Los Angeles Police Department." Douglas asked why he was calling on his fiancée's phone Sgt. Pollack said they found several phones at an accident site today.

"We're making calls from all the phones. You left a voice mail a while ago and you were the last number dialed on this phone." Douglas explained that the phone belonged to Devin Clark. "Is she okay?" Sgt. Pollack didn't know. "I think that most of the people involved in the accident were taken to the California Medical Center. Douglas asked if she was at Cal-Med. The sergeant didn't know for sure. "Sorry I can't be more help. I'm tagging and bagging the phones and all the personal belongings. You can pick them up at the shuttle company office."

Douglas hung up and told Marge what had happened. "I'll call you from the car." The stop-and-start traffic on the way to Westwood was not helping his state of mind. He called Marge and asked her to look on his desk for Mary Clark's phone number. "See if you can find the number and text it to my phone." She told him she would, "Don't drive crazy and get into an accident." Douglas said he would drive safely, as he honked his horn at a slow-moving car. Marge knew he was speeding. "I'll be here if you need me, just call!"

Douglas weaved in and out of traffic trying to pick the best lane. He was exceeding the speed limit when possible and at one point almost drove on the sidewalk. He was less than calm when he arrived at the California Medical Center. He parked and speed-walked to the main reception desk where he had to nervously wait in a short line It was just after four-thirty PM when he finally got to the desk.

He showed his business card. "Hello, I'm Douglas Hedges. I'm trying to find information on my fiancée, Devin Clark. She was involved in an accident today on the 405 freeway." The desk clerk checked her computer. "I don't see a Devin Clark. I don't see that anyone named Clark was admitted today" She checked another screen.

"There are several Jane Doe's. Perhaps she could be one of those. Check with the Intensive Care Unit on the third floor." Douglas thanked her and crossed the lobby to the elevators. Finding a big crowd outside the elevator he looked for the stairs and bounded up the three flights. Passing a nurse in the hallway, he asked for directions to the ICU desk. She pointed the way and Douglas tried to calm himself as he walked up to the nurse's station. A cheerful face greeted him, "Yes sir, may I help you?"

Douglas showed his business card again as he explained who he was looking for. The main desk nurse scanned her computer and said, "There are several Jane Doe's in the system, but no Clark's. Two of them are in our Intensive Care Unit." Douglas explained that Devin was his fiancée and he was also her attorney. "Would it be possible to see the Jane Doe's?" The nurse looked at his very fancy card and said, "Yes Mr. Hedges that can be arranged. She called for assistance and a young orderly appeared.

"Please take Mr. Hedges to see the two Jane Doe's in ICU. He's looking for his fiancée. Stay with him, please." The orderly put on a small white mask and handed one to Douglas as they entered the intensive care unit. They walked quietly as Douglas looked at a sleeping, elderly lady in bed #1. He shook his head, no. The second Jane Doe was also sleeping, but that wasn't her either. Douglas removed his mask and said, "Thank you, I guess Devin isn't here."

Chapter 20

A Waiting Game

Douglas thanked the orderly again and approached the ICU desk. The nurse asked, "Was she there?" He quietly said, "No. I didn't see her and I don't know where else to look. Are there any other locations where people might have been taken?" The nurse told him if the accident happened on the 405, they would have been brought here. She lowered her tone as she added, "If they were deceased, they'd be in our morgue. But even those names would be listed in our computer system. She's not here, sir." Douglas thanked the staff for their help and took a seat in the hallway across from the desk.

He was beside himself as he called Marge. "I'm at Cal-Med, but I can't find her. They haven't admitted anybody named Clark today." Marge asked if there were any Jane Doe's? He told her about the two he saw, "Neither one of them was her. I should call her parents, I know they're worried, but I don't know what to say. I'll hang here for a while." Douglas sat starring into space, not knowing what to do next. He was about to dial Devin's parents when a nurse handed him a note. "Mr. Hedges, this is from a lady in the intensive care unit. She can't speak, but it seems she heard your voice."

Douglas smiled as he looked at the note. **"Douglas, I'm here. I can't talk, come get me - D."** With tears in his eyes he said, "It's from Devin, where is she?" The nurse motioned for him to follow her. "We have her listed under another name. I'll have to find out why."

They entered the Intensive Care Unit and moved to the very last bed. The nurse slid the curtain back and Douglas cracked his first smile of the day. He looked at the nurse, "This isn't a Jane Doe. This is Miss Devin Clark." The nurse made a note. He couldn't wipe the smile off his face, "She's soon to be Mrs. Devin Hedges." The nurse smiled at the lady in the bed. "Nice to meet you Miss Clark. We'll be moving you to another room very soon, but first I've got some things to straighten out." She asked Douglas to see her at the desk as she left them holding hands.

Douglas looked down at his beautiful lady with such a sense of relief. He leaned over and kissed her gently on the forehead and told her there was nothing to worry about now. "I'm not leaving. I'll be outside, finding out what happened." She whispered, "Thank you."

Douglas looked back at his lady, "I'm going to call your parents. Just rest now; I'll be back."

He left the ICU and immediately called Devin's parents on the East Coast to give them a complete rundown. "She's fine, and I'll make sure she calls you as soon as she can." Douglas also called Marge again. "I'll be staying here tonight and might not be around tomorrow." She told him not to worry. "I'll handle everything on this end."

Douglas went to the nurses' station and told them that Devin was whispering. The nurse smiled and said, "That was a good sign. We'll be moving her to different room now. The doctor needs to do some tests." Douglas wondered why they had her listed under another name. The nurse explained that when people from the accident were brought in, it was a chaotic scene. "Many of them were unconscious. It seems she had a purse on her stretcher. I guess it was found at the accident scene, and they must have thought it was hers. It actually belongs to a woman in our morgue." Douglas was sorry to hear the news but glad they figured it out. The nurse asked if he knew the name of Devin's insurance company. He didn't know. "I'll be taking care of all charges. Here's my credit card."

The nurse entered his information into her computer. "I'll check with the doctor for you about her tests. We should have the results soon." Douglas plopped himself down in the waiting room. He was thinking back over the events of the day and the past year when his cell phone rang. He saw the caller's name on the screen. "Hi Bernie." The very agitated caller said he just heard from their office in Florida, "Devin never arrived!" Douglas calmed him down as he brought him up to speed. "I'm with her now at the hospital." Bernie decided right then, not to have Devin return to Florida. Bernie said, "I'm making a command decision. She'll be taking over our West Coast offices now, instead of July.

Somebody else will run Florida." Bernice agreed with that decision and both sent their regards. "If you need anything, call us." Douglas sat in the quiet waiting area and was starting to slip into a light snooze when someone gently tapped him on the shoulder.

"Mr. Hedges? I'm Doctor Stevens. We just finished some tests on Miss Clark. Both the MRI and CAT scan were negative and everything else looks fine." Douglas was very happy to hear that news. The doctor took the chair next to Douglas. "She did hit her forehead in the accident so, there will most-likely be headaches and some blurred vision. But those will pass quickly. She also fractured her left forearm and we're fitting her with a cast as we speak." He told Douglas they would have a prescription for her and she should be discharged within the hour or so. Douglas thanked the doctor and told him, "I'll be sitting right here."

He called Marge at home and gave her the good news. It was already past two AM in Connecticut, when Douglas called the Clarks. Mrs. Clark was very relieved to hear that Devin was well-enough to be released. She was also excited about her new West Coast job. She asked Douglas to have Devin call them tomorrow. "I will Mrs. Clark." Her response made Douglas smile, "Call me Mary or Mom, either one is acceptable." Douglas was touched by the statement and quietly said, "Good night Mom." He smiled as he settled back into the waiting room chair and closed his eyes.

Less than an hour later a soft voice asked, "Are you Mr. Hedges?" He sat up, looked around and realized that he'd been sleeping. "Yes I am." The night nurse told him that his wife would be ready to leave very soon. Douglas began to smile, *"my wife,"* he thought, *that's right!* It was way past midnight when they rolled Devin into the reception area. She signed some papers and the orderly pushed her wheel chair to the elevator. Devin was sleepy as she hugged the arm of her "husband." Douglas waved, thanked the nurses and said goodnight. He brought the car around and the orderly helped Devin into the passenger's seat. She winced and managed to say a very soft, "Thank you."

Devin didn't remember much about what happened. She was still whispering as she said that she was talking to a lady in the shuttle when she heard a crash and then the van rolled over. "The next thing I remember was waking up in the hospital." Douglas reminded her to rest her voice. He said, 'I spoke to your parents. They're glad you're okay, they want you to call them tomorrow." He looked at the dashboard clock. "It's already tomorrow. Call them later today. I also spoke with Bernie and Bernice and you're taking over the West Coast operation tomorrow, or rather today instead of July." Devin was all-smiles as she tried to say, "You mean I don't have to live in Florida anymore?" Douglas looked over at his lady in the cast. "No, you're moving in with me. Bernie's going to have the Florida office ship all your stuff here. You're mine, lady! I've got to nurse you back to health."

Devin held up the cast slightly and whispered. "At least this time, the cast is on my left-arm, so I can still draw. Is it too late to call Shelly?" Douglas thought about it and said, "No, Shelly's a night owl. Are you sure you're up to it?" Devin laughed, "I'll be ok. Shelly used to be a night owl, but then she got married."

She called her anyway and talked softly. The girls chatted all the way back to the condo. Douglas smiled as he listened to them gossip and carry on. Devin put the call on speaker as she said, "Douglas, Shelly wants to know when we're getting married?" He yelled at the phone, "I don't think people can get married wearing a cast." Devin took the phone off speaker, "He's right, I have at least 6 weeks in this stupid cast. That's lots of time for us to plan the perfect wedding."

They reached the condo and Douglas helped Devin into the elevator. She was a little wobbly and once inside Douglas directed her to the bedroom. He told her that he'd find her purse and suitcase tomorrow at the shuttle company. She yawned and said she was tired. "I'm a little hungry, but I'll have a big breakfast in the morning." Douglas helped her into bed and let out a big sigh of relief.

She motioned with her hand and said, "Come here for a moment." Douglas turned to her. "Sure, what do you need?" She held out her good arm, "I need a goodnight kiss from my future husband." Douglas smiled and moved to the side of the bed. "Okay, I can do that." He kissed her and she snuggled into the light covers.

Douglas went to his well-stocked bar and fixed a large gin and tonic, because it had been a very long, stressful day and night. He sat on the couch looking through the open bedroom door. He thought, *"What a difference a day makes!"* Devin was soon fast asleep. Her left arm might have been in a cast, but she was still wearing her engagement ring. One of the nurses said she told the Doctor, that she was keeping her ring on, because it took her a long time to find the right guy. Douglas felt great to know that *he* was the right guy!

Chapter 21

March Came in Like a Lion

After several days of R & R, Devin was up and around and ready to get back to work. Douglas found her suitcase, purse and phone at the shuttle company and B & B arranged for her "stuff" to be packed and shipped from Florida. She also gave notice at her Silver Lake apartment and she and Shelly set out to pack and clean up the old place.

During her six-week recovery Douglas would drop Devin off at B & B's office in down town Los Angeles every morning and pick her up in the evening. When the cast was removed, it was the same routine as last year; some physical therapy, then she would drive her VW to the office.

Things were going well and Douglas was beginning to feel a little "married." Each morning they had breakfast, or at least coffee together and dinner at the same table most evenings. Some of her free time seemed to be consumed with bridal magazines. It was like planning the Battle of Normandy with Shelly as the General. There were occasional trips to the mall and visits with Douglas' family in San Diego. During a quiet moment, Devin did some on-line research and one evening when Douglas arrived at the condo, she showed him what she'd been doing.

"Look what I did today." She handed him a printout. "I filled out the marriage license application on-line. All we do is appear in person, pay about ninety-dollars and we get our license." Douglas looked over the papers. "Ninety-Dollars? I don't know, that sounds like a deal-breaker to me." Devin joined him kidding around. "Sure, you lead a girl on and then won't pop for ninety-bucks." She grabbed her purse and removed some money. "Here's a hundred, keep the change. Can we go tomorrow to get the license?" He kissed her and agreed that it was a good idea, "Let's get it early on the way to work."

Now that they had that settled, Devin could concentrate on getting B & B's next fashion show up and running. She told Douglas a little about the new show in downtown toward the end of March. B & B would only be showing her designs. She was working on drawing a logo, but needed help to get her trademark established and a lot of other "legal stuff." Douglas laughed, "So, now the truth comes out, you only love me for my legal mind." She moved close to him, "And you only love me because of my sexy designs and my legs." She raised her dress and gave him a look. Douglas starred at her beautifully tanned legs, "Your honor, both statements are out of order. She's trying to lead the witness." Devin kissed him on the forehead and dragged him to the living room which smelled like an Italian restaurant. They spent a quiet evening at home snuggling in front of the big-screen

TV eating pizza from Village Pizza. The box said, *"Our pizza is the best in town."* They agreed, it was great!

The next morning, they were in line at the county clerk's office and got to the window after just a thirty-minute wait. Devin had everything ready. They each produced a photo ID, raised their right hands, paid the ninety-bucks and received a license. They went to their respective jobs, each smiling, when nobody was looking.

The Devin Designs Fashion Show was set for the last Friday in March at B & B's downtown loft warehouse. Devin and Shelly were working hard to get things arranged. The condo became ground-zero for the show. In the second bedroom, they had several white boards with post-it-notes and reminders. They also had material swatches, model photos and a million other things. Douglas looked in, saw the mess, and closed the door. This was her project; he didn't want to get in the way.

They also had a stack of invitations, stamps, and mailing labels on the desk in the living room. Shelly saw Douglas looking around and told him not to worry about the mess. "Soon, all of these things will be going to B & B's office. You won't even know it was here." Devin looked up from the couch, "Yes, we'll be moving everything soon. I made some space at B & B." Douglas told them he wasn't worried, "Your old apartment always got cleaned up after somebody we know poured beer, opened cans of pet food and worked on many other projects." The girls laughed, but had to agree that Shelly always cleaned up her sloppiness.

Douglas told them that he'd worked out all the details for the expansion of the business, "Your trademarks, the website, the contracts, plans, everything. Bring B & B over to the office tomorrow and we'll get it all signed." Devin kissed him on the cheek. "Yes, husband-to-be." Douglas looked over the stack of invitations and asked, "When does this new project launch?" Devin told him they would have all the answers right after the fashion show. "B and B want to see how the sales go before they announce the expansion."

Justin dropped by to pick up Shelly and once again, Douglas and Devin settled in for a nice evening of TV and a wonderful foot massage. Douglas was keeping very busy at the office. He was starting early and leaving at a decent time. His billable hours were way up and he didn't have time to think about a lot of other things. Marge entered with the B & B file. Douglas reviewed everything and told her it was ready for signatures. She set the meeting for later that day. Marge, once again, asked about the wedding. Douglas really hadn't given it a thought.

B & B and Devin appeared on time, they looked over everything, and found all the papers were, as expected, correct. Douglas was very happy about the new direction the company was about to take. He was glad that B & B was going from a small Mom & Pop shop to a bicoastal operation. He was also delighted at the way they added Devin Designs into their product line. She was connected and yet separate in case she wanted to branch out on her own later. Everyone signed on the dotted lines as Marge entered with some special mango-pineapple ice tea.

Bernie thanked Marge and asked if she was coming to their fashion show. She told them she had it on her calendar. "Bring your husband too. We'll have an open bar, a light dinner, dancing, it's gonna be fun." Marge smiled and said, "Yes, we'll be there. When Ralph hears free food and booze, I won't be able to keep him away." Devin took Douglas' arm. "You'll be there, right?" He smiled and said, "Of course. I want a reserved seat in the front row." Bernie told him, "We have the Florida office staff coming, reps from the manufacturing company, buyers from all the major chains and of course a whole bunch of helpers to take orders." Bernice told him, "It's going to be bigger than our last show, because now we have Devin's Designs." Bernie, Bernice and Devin were very relieved that everything was finished. Devin thanked Marge and then hugged Douglas, "I'll see you at home." Douglas hugged her back, "Yes, you will. Let's celebrate tonight."

Douglas closed his office and stopped at the florist in the lobby. He thought a nice bouquet and some wine were the perfect choices to celebrate the birth of her new business. She kissed him as soon as he got home and loved the flowers which she placed in the center of the dining room table. He opened the bottle of wine and they toasted poolside on the upper deck.

Devin loved to swim and since the pool was built by Douglas and totally isolated from view, they both swam sans swimwear. It was an adventurous celebration which continued until the wee hours of the morning. They ended the night soaking wet and totally expended.

March was super busy. There was a lot of business for Douglas and a flurry of activity for Devin. The days were moving quickly and all they were seeing of each other was a glimpse at breakfast and a foot or back rub at night. They both decided that after the fashion show, they would each take some vacation time. When Douglas mentioned that he *might* be taking a "real vacation" after the fashion show, Marge kicked into high-gear. She loaded him up with every travel brochure she could carry.

Douglas looked at the stack of leaflets, "Where did you get all this stuff?" Marge shook her head in disbelief, "Downstairs, at the travel agency in the lobby." He didn't acknowledge anything. "You mean you've been in this building for all these years and didn't know there was a travel agency on the ground floor?" Douglas starred at the colorful flyers. "I've only come in the front door a few times, and just didn't notice, I guess." Marge agreed, "And since you don't go out to lunch, it makes sense. Remember, you have that fashion show tomorrow at four."

Douglas put a handful of the brochures in his briefcase. He noticed that it was getting dark outside. He thought *"either the days are getting shorter or I'm working so much they just seem shorter."* He called Devin who was already at the condo with dinner ready. He asked if she needed anything for her big day tomorrow. She said," No, it's all taken care of." When Douglas arrived home, he didn't recognize the place. When he left that morning, there were reminders of the fashion show all over. Pieces of fabric on the desk and scraps of sticky paper posted everywhere. He looked around as if he was in the wrong house. "Okay. I give up what have you done with my fiancée? You know who I'm talking about, the one that makes a mess."

Devin met up with him and gave him a gigantic hug and kiss. "Shelly and I cleaned it all up and moved everything to B & B. I need it all there, not here."

Douglas noticed that she was very calm and collected. "You sure everything is ready for tomorrow?" She kissed him, "Yes, why do you ask?" He looked at her, "Because last time, I seem to recall a slightly different Devin Clark." She motioned to him to follow her to the kitchen. "This time I have a staff. B & B have gone out of their way to make this a truly fantastic show. I can't wait. We have valet parking, cocktails at four. The big show and a light dinner after. We have people to take orders, too. We've thought of everything!"

Douglas was very happy to hear that things were going to be perfect. "Well, that's wonderful! Speaking of wonderful, what do I smell? Can you cook?"

Devin smiled and made a grand gesture, "Yes, I can cook. I tossed together a little Chicken Parmesan, Penne Pasta and a salad. Nothing that any world-class fashion designer couldn't handle. They're Tony's recipes." Douglas hugged her, "I'm so proud of you! I'm going to wear an extra-large shirt, because my chest is going to be so pumped up for you." Douglas started to kiss her and the cook stopped him by putting a large serving spoon on his lips. "Let's eat. You can kiss me all night if you like, after we eat." He took his seat at the table and sat quietly as she put a large platter in front of him. "Douglas, I think we should go swimming again tonight." That put a smile on his face for the entire dinner which was, first-class.

He wondered how she learned to cook, but she wouldn't tell him. "Did your mother teach you?" She still didn't answer. She just told him to take his drink and follow her to the pool. They relaxed poolside with their after-dinner drinks. Douglas said, "If you ever want to change professions, try opening a restaurant!" She laughed, "No, that's too much work. Here's a question. How did you get this pool built up here on the roof?"

Douglas shrugged, "It was no big deal. Nothing that any world-class lawyer and his over-stuffed checkbook couldn't handle. I got the zoning change, gave all the other owners a little something to compensate for the noise and dust and soon half of it will be yours." She loved that idea. "Oh, I never thought of that. Let's get wet." They really tired each other out during their "swim." They both found that making love in the pool was a bit more exciting than they realized. As a result, they ended the night even more exhausted. They fell asleep in each other's arms while watching the late, late show on the bedroom television.

Chapter 22

Fashion Show Friday

It was Fashion Show Friday and Devin was the first up and out of the condo very early. She kissed Douglas and reminded him that today was the big show. "See you this afternoon." He told her he and Marge would be there. "Have a great show!"

Douglas was still tired, but a wonderful shower brought him back to life. He dressed and left the house in a hurry forgetting his change of clothes for the fashion show. The office was unusually busy for a Friday which made three-thirty roll around super-fast! Douglas was out of his office, on time, heading toward B & B's loft. Marge left just before two o'clock because she wanted to go home, change, and pick up her husband. When Douglas arrived, the valet took his car and parked it in the #1 spot, just off the door! *That's great service,* Douglas thought as he met up with Bernie & Bernice at the entrance. They introduced him to a few friends and then Douglas saw the Florida staff. There were hugs all around as he said, "Welcome to California." Bernice removed the "reserved' sign and dusted off a chair. "As promised, a front row seat. Here's a program." Douglas thanked Bernice and began to look around the loft. It was beautifully decorated.

He turned his attention to the program and started reading Devin's bio. He found out that she used to twirl the baton at high-school football games, and was a medal-winning sprinter and also learned that she studied culinary arts in college. Douglas smiled and thought, *No wonder she can cook*. He thought the stage was very professionally designed and constructed with four heavy-duty light towers. Each had a dozen or so chrome-plated stage lights. He thought, *this is just like a rock concert*. Marge & Ralph arrived. Marge looked great, "Is that a new dress?" She smiled and said, "Yes, because this is a special occasion." Marge looked him over. "Is that the same suit you had on at the office? You didn't change?"

Douglas suddenly felt underdressed. "I had some clothes at the condo, but I forgot them. I didn't think it was necessary to change. You've seen how people come dressed to these things." Marge dusted off his shoulder and fixed his tie. "Maybe you're right, you look okay." Ralph shook hands with Douglas, "I heard they have food today." Douglas smiled and indicated the bar area, "Yes, food and an open bar." Ralph started off, "I think I'd like a beer. Anything for you guys?" They both said, "No, we're fine." Marge watched as her husband made his way to the bar, "Ralph is a sweet man; he loves me and beer."

Douglas showed the program to Marge, "I just found out that Devin was a baton twirler in high-school." She smiled and said, "I'll bet you'll find out lots of stuff about each other over time." When Ralph returned, Douglas noticed that the place was almost full. Shelly & Justin took the two reserved seats next to

Douglas and she said, "Isn't this exciting, her own line of fashions. I'm so happy for her, and you."

The lights dimmed slightly and then the room went dark. The up-tempo music started and several colorful spotlights began to circle the audience and stage. The announcer welcomed everyone. "Ladies and Gentlemen B & B Fashions present their new line of resort wear. These are Devin Designs!" The music swelled and Devin's new LOGO changed from white to bright red. There was applause as the first of twelve beautiful models made her way onto the runway. The announcer did a wonderful job with each description. The show was flowing well and the applause level was increasing. The designs were simply sensational!

It was very inspired work which Devin had kept under wraps for months. Slimming swim fashions, that could double as evening wear. Also, a new line of high-fashion resort wear for men and women. Douglas leaned over to Marge, "I can tell this is a hit!" The announcer said, "And finally, please meet our newest designer. Here's Devin!"

Douglas' fiancée accompanied by all twelve of her models, appeared on-stage. Devin wore a white-on-white, off-the-shoulder evening gown with embroidered palm trees that gave it a tropical flair. Her entrance and original design really capped off the show. Devin hugged each model and acknowledged the applause.

The announcer continued, "Ladies and Gentlemen, this is a special occasion! You're seeing Devin's Designs for the first time, anywhere." He paused and ended his commentary, "If you would like to order any of the fashions you've seen today, please see one of our representatives in the lobby." He handed a microphone to Devin. She smiled and looked all around the building. "I want to thank all of you for coming and because this is a premier and a very special occasion, I want to offer you a twenty-five percent discount on all orders placed tonight!" There was a burst of applause, as the lighting changed to a subtle pink glow and a man in a stylish tuxedo appeared on stage behind the models. Devin nodded and the models moved to both sides of the runway. She approached the mystery man and put a red rose in the button hole of his lapel. A hush fell over the audience.

The man in black said, "Who is being married here today?" Devin smiled, "I am! I'm Devin Clark." The man in the tux looked at Devin, "Miss Clark, who are you marrying?" Devin extended her hand and pointed as she said, "This man, Douglas Hedges." Shelly and Marge pushed the shocked and embarrassed lawyer up. Shelly said, "You're on Douglas." Devin took his hand, pulled him on stage as the audience applauded. She guided him toward the minister who said, "Devin Clark & Douglas Hedges this is your special day. Who gives this woman to be married to this man?" From the back of the room Mary & Charles Clark moved forward and stepped on the runway saying, "We do." Douglas was surprised and delighted to see them.

The minister continued, "Devin & Douglas, we have come together before God, your families and friends to unite you in Holy Matrimony. I'm sure this was a surprise to you, Douglas, I can see it on your face." The audience laughed and applauded. Douglas laughed too and said, "Is this real? Are you a real minister?" The tall man in black smiled and said, "Yes sir. I am and it's time! Please join hands."

The minister launched into the standard text of the ceremony, heard them both say "I do" and moved on asking for the rings. Marge stood and handed the rings to one of the models who then gave them to the minister. The minister continued the ceremony with the traditional dialogue. "With this ring, I thee wed." With both rings on their fingers, the minister asked Devin if she had anything she wanted to say. She had prepared and memorized a short statement.

"Douglas, I've known you for a year and a few months. Four-hundred-fifty-five days to be exact. I knew I loved you several months after we first met, but for some reason, I waited to tell you. Now I can't wait to start our new life together and I promise that I will love you more every day." She smiled and looked at the Minister who then turned to Douglas. "I know you didn't prepare anything Douglas, because you really didn't know this was going to happen, but would you care to say a few words?" Douglas thought for a moment and looked in Devin's eyes and nodded yes.

"I fell in love with you Miss Clark the first day I saw you, which according to your math was four-hundred-fifty-five days ago. I was waiting for the right moment to tell you how I felt and that moment came when we danced at Shelly's engagement party. I promise to love you more every single day!" Douglas looked down at Shelly who was sobbing and then turned to the minister who smiled and said, "Then by the authority vested in me by the State of California, I now pronounce you husband and wife. You may kiss your bride!"

The newlyweds kissed and the loft erupted in laughter and applause. They thanked the minister and exited the stage as the DJ played an updated version of the classic wedding conclusion song, "Mendelssohn's Wedding March." Douglas helped his bride down the steps and into the waiting arms of their family and friends. There were hugs from Marge, Shelly, Bernie, Bernice, Devin's parents and then Douglas turned to see his crying mom and sniffling father. Brother Michael congratulated him too, but had to whisper, "I'll get you for this."

Devin asked if her husband had anything to say. "I am totally speechless, Mrs. Hedges." They kissed lightly. Marge laughed and said, "That's a first! I never saw that happen before— Douglas with nothing to say!" The party continued with the bride and groom making the rounds. Devin and Douglas moved to the DJ's microphone and thanked everyone for coming then said, "I also want to thank B & B fashions for believing in my designs. Remember in honor of our wedding, that Douglas really didn't know about, all orders will be discounted twenty-five percent. The DJ took his mic and said, "It's time for the happy couple's first dance! I know what to play."

He started the instrumental version of "Loves Theme." Douglas and Devin kissed lightly and started to dance. As they swayed, Devin wanted to know if he was mad at her. He didn't understand the question, "Mad? Why?" Devin asked, "Because you got roped into this?" He smiled and told her he wanted to marry her from the first time he saw her in a cast at the impound lot and the second time he saw her in a cast at the hospital.

They kissed as he said, "Promise me you won't break anything again." The DJ asked everyone to join the happy couple, "Let's all dance." The floor filled quickly with family and friends. Douglas looked around to see many smiling faces including Mr. Lawson and his wife. They dropped by because Marge told them what was going to happen. Devin left Douglas to dance with her dad who was both happy and sad at the same time. Douglas did a few steps with Devin's mom. They both switched to dance with Doug's mom and dad and then all six came together for a group hug.

Shelly made sure that everyone in the room had a flute filled with champagne to toast the happy couple. She also picked the perfect cake which was so good everyone wanted the name of the bakery. For a "surprise party" it was well-planned and executed perfectly. Several wanted to know the name of their party consultant. Devin pointed them to Shelly. B & B were very busy helping their staff with orders. The entire line was selling. They ran to Devin to give her the good news. She was overjoyed and started to cry. "Wow, they really like my designs." Bernice hugged her, "You're a hit and you're married!"

Douglas hugged his crying wife. "I'm delighted that the show went so well and that your designs are selling. Congratulations, Mrs. Hedges." He raised his glass and took a sip of his champagne. "So, where are we going for our honeymoon?" Devin looked at her husband, "That's up to you. You're the man of the house. Make a decision."

The family all agreed and yelled, "DOUGLAS, MAKE A DECISION!" But he didn't have an answer because he didn't know he was getting married. Marge slipped Douglas two airline tickets behind his back and whispered, "I used your credit card, again." Douglas laughed and looked at Devin as he said, "Okay, I've made a decision." He held up the tickets, "As the first official act as the man of the house, I'll tell you that we're going to, to…" He paused and fumbled with the tickets Marge came to his rescue and blurted out the answer. "Hawaii!" Douglas glanced at the tickets, "Yes, Hawaii."

He hugged Marge and kissed her on the cheek. "Thank you again." Devin was all-smiles, "Not bad, Mr. H." Douglas hugged her too, "Thank you Mrs. H. We also need to thank Marge!" Devin hugged and thanked a tearful Marge who said, "Don't mind me, I always cry at wedding receptions." Devin grabbed Douglas, "Let's dance husband. Next stop Hawaii."

The next day as they were packing for their big trip, they received a special delivery. Devin tore open the box to find Tony's cookbook. They loved the sunset on the cover. She read the card out loud. "Congratulations! I knew you would be together the first time I saw you at the Grotto. Drop by anytime. Dinner is always FREE to family!" Douglas joined her on the couch as they thumbed thru the book. The dedication read:

GRAZIE to My family and to Douglas, Devin, Marge, Shelly and all my Loyal Customers

Chapter 23

Never Too Late for Love

During their honeymoon trip, Mr. and Mrs. Hedges uploaded photos to their social media pages. There were pictures of them at a luau and on a moonlight dinner cruise. There were several out-of-breath shots as they climbed Diamond Head. Devin also got some photos of Douglas, "chicken-legs" Hedges learning to surf. Those pictures only went to his family. Devin was always scouring gift shops to pick out the perfect card. Yes, they acted like typical tourists as they mailed beautiful picture postcards to:

Mary & Charles Clark
Sonya & William Hedgegroves
Shelly & Justin
Marge & Ralph
Bernie & Bernice
The Lawson Legal Group - office staff
Devin Designs - office staff

These cards said

"Having a Great Time - See you Soon!"

The also sent cards to
Billy @ The Village Tavern - Dr. Martha English and
Tony @ The Italian Grotto
Douglas added this note

"Having a great time. Sorry, I didn't invite you to the wedding, but I didn't know I was getting married! Remember, Devin LOVES to surprise me!"

The following year, Devin expanded her clothing line to include resort fashions for children. The expansion coincided with the sending of the following announcement.

We are delighted to announce
the birth of our daugher
Allison Louise Hedges
7 lbs. 3 oz. of joy came into
our lives on July 4th.
Always FIREWORKS on her birthday!
Devin & Douglas Hedges

Devin established the perfect niche for her clothing line. Along the way, she won many awards for her innovative designs. Her greatest awards however, always come from the smiles of little Allison and the accolades from her adoring husband. Douglas left his annual bonus in the dust and opened his own small office in the Village. Marge came with him of course, because he never did understand the computer or the intercom.

The Hedges' share office space these days just a short walk from their West L.A. condo. The quaint Village has everything, including a pre-school which will come in handy in a few years. Right now, baby Ally rolls to work with Mommy and has plenty of "extra" relatives to tend to her every need. There's Auntie Marge, Auntie Bernice & Uncle Bernie.

Most nights the Hedges family can be found in front of the big screen TV. Douglas hung his gift plaque on the living room wall and now realizes that he did GET A LIFE. Each time he looks over at the two "sofa rats," as he calls them, he knows that it really is

NEVER TOO LATE FOR LOVE!

Chapter 24

Sunset at the Grotto

Ever since they received Tony's book, Devin and Douglas spend a lot of time cooking together. The book holds a place of honor in their kitchen. Following are a few of the recipes they enjoy from: **SUNSET AT THE GROTTO - A Collection of Tony's Favorites**

ANTIPASTO SALAD

Ingredients

1 small clove garlic, finely chopped
2 tablespoons balsamic vinegar
¼ cup extra virgin olive oil
2 tablespoons chopped fresh basil
Salt and freshly ground black pepper
1 (6 ounce) jar marinated artichoke hearts, cut in halves
4 ounces whole milk Mozzarella cheese, cut into ½-inch cubes
½ cup thinly sliced red onion
8-10 Roma tomatoes, cut in chunks
12 large pitted black olives
6-8 pepperoncini peppers
3 ounces light dry salami or ham, cut into strips
½ medium red bell pepper, cut into thin strips

Instructions

Use a whisk to mix garlic, vinegar, and oil in a small bowl. Add basil and season to taste with salt and pepper. Add rest of the ingredients to the vinaigrette and toss to coat.

Place chopped lettuce on a large platter. Place everything on top of lettuce and enjoy!

"We really enjoy this salad especially on warm evenings on our patio. It's really a complete meal." Devin & Douglas.

BRUSCHETTA SUPREME

Ingredients

6 Roma tomatoes, seeded and chopped
½ cup shredded fresh Parmesan cheese *(it's easier to grate when frozen)*
1 cup cubed Mozzarella cheese
¼ cup minced fresh basil
2 tablespoons minced fresh parsley
4 garlic cloves, finely minced
2 teaspoons balsamic vinegar
⅛ teaspoon salt
⅛ teaspoon crushed red pepper flakes
⅛ teaspoon pepper
1 French bread baguette, cut into ½-inch slices and spread with olive oil

Instructions

In a medium-sized bowl, combine all the ingredients except bread and olive oil.

Lightly spread bread slices with olive oil. Place on ungreased baking sheets and broil until lightly toasted. You can also toast bread slices, then spread with olive oil. With a slotted spoon, top each slice with tomato mixture.

"Oh my, our friends beg us to make this appetizer whenever we get together. It's the best!" **Shelly & Jason.**

"Ralph eats this as if it's potato chips—he can't just eat one!" **Marge**

BAKED CHICKEN PARMESAN

(a quick & simple recipe)

Ingredients

4 boneless skinless chicken breasts

1 lightly beaten egg

¼ cup 2% milk

½ cup fresh grated Parmesan cheese (freezing makes the cheese easier to grate)

1 cup Italian seasoned bread crumbs

2-3 cups Tony's Marinara or Spaghetti Sauce

1 cup shredded Mozzarella cheese

Instructions

Preheat oven to 400 degrees F.

Combine lightly beaten egg and milk in a bowl.

Dip chicken in egg/milk mixture. Dip in Parmesan and breadcrumb mixture. Be sure chicken pieces are well-coated. Place breaded chicken breasts in a 13x9 inch glass baking dish.

Bake uncovered for 20 minutes. Pour sauce over chicken and top with shredded Mozzarella cheese. Bake an additional 10 minutes or until done. Check with an instant read thermometer. Internal temp should be 165 degrees F when done.

"Oh my, such a simple recipe and so delicious. Jason has made it a few times already." Shelly & Jason

TONY'S FAMOUS ITALIAN SPAGHETTI SAUCE

(This sauce is best on the second day)

Ingredients

1 (28 oz.) can tomato puree
1 (12 oz.) can tomato paste
2 (28 oz.) cans crushed tomatoes
1 cup finely chopped onion
4 garlic cloves, crushed
4 Tbs. olive oil
1 tsp. salt
1 tsp. freshly ground pepper
1 Tbs. dried basil
1 tsp. dried oregano
½ tsp. dried thyme leaves
½ tsp. dried rosemary leaves
¼ cup fresh Parmesan cheese
½ cup red wine
2 ½ cups water

Instructions

In a large pot on low heat, sauté onions in olive oil for about 4-5 minutes. Add crushed garlic and cook for 2 minutes longer. Add water and all the tomato products. Mix well. Add spices and bring to a boil. Add Parmesan cheese. Cover pot and reduce heat and simmer for 2 ½ hours. Add wine and continue to simmer for 30 minutes longer. Sauce will be thin on first day. If you use meat, brown first. It will make sauce thicker. On the second day this turns into a nice thick sauce.

"I have several quart jars of this delicious sauce in the freezer. We love it!" Devin & Douglas.

LUSCIOUS HOT FUDGE CAKE

This is a rich, chocolate cake that's not overly sweet. Serve with a scoop of ice cream or whipped cream over top and enjoy!

Ingredients

1 cup all-purpose flour
¾ cup white sugar
2 Tbs. unsweetened cocoa powder
2 tsp. baking powder
½ cup milk
2 Tbs. vegetable oil
1 tsp. vanilla

Instructions

Combine flour, sugar, cocoa, baking powder and salt. Stir in milk, oil and vanilla until smooth. Spread in ungreased 9-inch square baking pan.

Combine 1 cup brown sugar and 4 Tbs. unsweetened cocoa powder and sprinkle over cake batter. Pour 1 cup HOT water over all. DO NOT stir.

Bake at 350 degrees for 35-40 minutes. Serve warm.

"I took Devin's advice and bought your book. This recipe alone was worth it. It's like our dining room is our own Italian Grotto." **Dr. Martha**

SAUSAGE & PEPPERS

(For sandwiches or over pasta)

Ingredients

1 large sweet onion
2 red bell peppers
2 green bell peppers
¼ cup olive oil
Salt and freshly ground pepper to taste
4 links Italian Sausage, sweet or hot
1 cup of TONY'S MARINARA SAUCE
4 Italian or French rolls (if making sandwiches)

Instructions

Cut onions in half and slice, thinly, cross-wise.

Cut peppers in half and remove the stems, seeds and membranes. Slice into thin strips.

In a large heavy skillet, heat olive oil over medium-high heat. Add peppers and onions and season with salt and pepper. Add marinara sauce.

Lower heat to medium-low and cook stirring frequently until onions and peppers are semi-soft, 15-20 minutes.

Place the sausage directly on grill or griddle and cook, turning until browned on all sides. Slice the rolls for sandwiches and place a sausage link in each roll. Cover with a heaping portion of the peppers and onions.

This is delicious served over any type of pasta, especially Fusilli or Rotini

"I made this for a potluck at the Elks Club. Everyone went crazy." Shelly

VEGGIE LASAGNA

Ingredients

4 medium Zucchini, halved lengthwise and thinly sliced
1 (8-oz.) package fresh mushrooms, thinly sliced
2 cloves garlic, finely minced
Vegetable cooking spray
1 red bell pepper, chopped
1 yellow bell pepper, chopped
1 onion, chopped
½ teaspoon salt
1 ½ cups ricotta cheese
1 large egg
2 cups (8 oz.) shredded Mozzarella cheese, divided
½ cup freshly grated Parmesan cheese, divided
4-5 cups Marinara Sauce (see Tony's recipe)
1 (8-oz.) package no-boil lasagna noodles

Instructions

Preheat oven to 450°. Roast zucchini, mushrooms, and garlic in a baking pan coated with cooking spray for 12 to 14 minutes or until vegetables are crisp-tender. Stir once or twice while roasting. Repeat procedure with bell peppers and onion. Reduce oven temperature to 350°. Toss roasted vegetables and salt in a bowl.

Stir together ricotta cheese, egg, 1 ½ cups shredded Mozzarella cheese, and ¼ cup grated Parmesan cheese.

Spread 1 cup Marinara Sauce in a 13" x 9" baking dish coated with cooking spray. Top with 3 noodles, 1 cup sauce, one-third of ricotta mixture and one-third of vegetable mixture; repeat layers twice.

Top with remaining noodles and 1 cup sauce. Sprinkle with remaining ½ cup shredded mozzarella and ¼ cup grated Parmesan.

Cover dish and bake at 350° for 45 minutes. Uncover and bake 10 to15 minutes longer or until cheese is melted and golden. Let stand 10 minutes.

"Whenever we think "healthy", we make this. But guess what, healthy it's not, but delicious it is!" **Devin**

BEEF BRACIOLE
(Stuffed Italian Beef Rolls)

Ingredients

1 lb. top sirloin, cut into 4 thin slices approximately ⅓ inch thick

4 slices prosciutto

2 Tbs. grated Pecorino Romano cheese

2 garlic cloves, minced well

2 Tbs. finely chopped parsley,

2 Tbs. olive oil

1 medium onion, finely chopped

2 carrots, peeled and diced

2 celery stalks, diced

1 cup dry red wine

2 (28 oz.) cans imported Italian tomatoes

1 ¼ cups water

2 bay leaves

3 fresh basil leaves, torn into small pieces

Flour

Salt & pepper to taste

Instructions

Place each slice of beef between 2 sheets of plastic wrap and pound with a meat mallet until ¼ inch thick. Sprinkle with salt & pepper. Place a slice of prosciutto on each one.

Mix together the Pecorino Romano cheese, garlic and parsley and sprinkle evenly on top of the beef slices with prosciutto. Roll up the slices and tuck in the ends. Tie with kitchen string.

Heat the olive oil in a large sauce pan over medium heat. Place flour in a flat bowl and dredge the meat rolls, shaking off any excess flour. Cook until browned on all sides, about 15 minutes.

Remove from pan and set aside.

Add more olive oil to the pan if needed, then add the onion, carrots and celery. Cook until tender but not browned, about 10 minutes. Add the red wine and cook, stirring up any browned bits stuck to the bottom of the pan until reduced by half.

Crush the tomatoes with your hands or use blender and lightly chop. Add to the saucepan with water. Add the bay leaves and season with salt and pepper. Place the Braciole back into the sauce, turn heat to low and simmer until beef is tender 1 ½ hours. Remove and discard bay leaves.

Sprinkle the basil over the rolls, and simmer for 2 minutes longer. Transfer to serving plates and spoon the sauce over the top and serve.

"We've made this for Dr. Martha and her husband when they were here for dinner. They wanted the recipe, so we told them to buy your book." **Devin & Doug**

FRESH MARINARA SAUCE

(in only 30 minutes)

Makes approximately 1 quart

Ingredients

5 pounds ripe tomatoes
2 tablespoons extra-virgin olive oil
4 large cloves garlic, finely minced
1 bunch fresh herbs (do not chop—tie in bunch)
(use basil or a combination of basil, parsley, oregano, and thyme)
1 teaspoon sugar
½ teaspoon salt
Freshly ground black pepper
½ teaspoon balsamic vinegar
Crushed red pepper flakes, to taste (optional)
Additional fresh chopped herbs, to taste (optional)

Instructions

Cut tomatoes into small chunks. Use your hands to squeeze the tomatoes into smaller pieces. Do not drain. You could also place tomatoes in a blender until smooth. In a large pot set over low heat, sauté minced garlic in olive oil until softened. Add tomatoes and juices to pot and place fresh herb bunch on top. Reduce heat and cover pot. Simmer for 30 minutes, stirring occasionally.

When sauce has thickened and reduced, remove herb bunch. Stir in sugar, salt, pepper and balsamic vinegar. Taste and adjust seasonings if necessary. Some folks prefer to skip the sugar. If desired, add crushed red pepper flakes and additional fresh chopped herbs. Use an immersion blender to lightly puree sauce. A bit of tomato chunks should remain. Serve warm. Allow to cool before storing. Sauce will keep in refrigerator for up to a week. Sauce also freezes well.

"We enjoy dipping our pizza sticks or toasted French bread in this sauce, as well as on any kind of pasta." Marge & Ralph."

Douglas and I like this on The Grotto's meatballs and penne pasta." Devin

CLASSIC ITALIAN MEATBALLS GROTTO STYLE

Ingredients

4 eggs, slightly beaten

¼ cup water

1 cup buttermilk or 1 cup milk and 1 tsp. vinegar

1 ½ cups unseasoned bread crumbs - *(At the Grotto, we make our own)*

4 teaspoons minced garlic

1 medium onion, finely minced

1 cup fresh Italian parsley, chopped

1 cup grated fresh Parmesan cheese

1 tablespoon dried oregano

2 teaspoons kosher salt

1 tablespoon ground black pepper

1 ½ lbs. ground pork

3 lbs. ground beef *(85% lean is best)*

Instructions

Preheat oven to 375 degrees. Combine eggs, water, buttermilk and breadcrumbs in a bowl; let rest for 10 minutes. The mixture will thicken as the bread crumbs absorb the liquid. Add garlic, onion, parsley, cheese, oregano, salt, and pepper. Stir until combined. Combine ground pork and beef in a large bowl.

Lightly mix meat mixture with fingers or a large fork only until meats are well-combined. Add bread crumb mixture to meats. Lightly mix these together. Combine ingredients well, but do not over mix. Form meatballs with hands or use a scoop. For larger meatballs, use ¼ cup meat per meatball or use a generous 2" scoop.

For mini meatballs, use 1 to 1 ½ tablespoons per meatball or a generous 1-¼" scoop. Place meatballs on baking sheets.

Bake large meatballs for 30 minutes and mini meatballs for 15 minutes, until no longer pink in center.

"After I made this the first time, I was hooked. So, I made a double batch and froze them. Now it's just thaw and serve as appetizers with your Marinara Sauce. - **Marge**

RICOTTA ZEPOLE

(Italian Fried Dessert)

Ingredients

2 eggs
2 tablespoon sugar
½ teaspoon vanilla extract
1 cup ricotta
1 cup all-purpose flour
2 teaspoons baking powder
¼ teaspoon of salt of salt
Vegetable oil for frying
Confectioners' sugar
Chocolate sauce or honey (optional)

Instructions

Combine the eggs, sugar and vanilla extract in a large bowl and whisk together. Stir in the ricotta cheese and mix until well combined.

In a separate bowl stir together the flour, baking powder and salt. Slowly add to the ricotta mixture and stir until a batter is formed.

In a deep saucepan, pour in vegetable oil to a depth of about 3 inches. Heat the oil to 370 degrees. (It's best to use a frying thermometer, instead of guessing)

Drop a heaping tablespoon of batter into the oil. Do not crowd the zepole in the pan. Make only 6 at a time. You can use a cookie scoop for this. Cook until golden brown and puffy, turning with a slotted spoon to fry evenly on all sides.

Drain zepole on paper towels. Sprinkle generously with powdered sugar and serve hot. Drizzle with chocolate ice-cream sauce or honey if desired.

"Yummy to the max!" Shelly

"Oh my, this is decadent, but wonderful." Devin

"The gang at the Elks Club said these are better than donuts and I agree." Shelly

About the Author

J.E. Duke is an Emmy Award-winning writer/producer who has worked in all phases of the entertainment industry. **"Never Too Late for Love"** is his first offering to the world of fiction.

Originally released as an E-Book only in 2009 under the title, *"Never Too Old for Love"* the story has since been expanded and updated. It is now available, for the first time, in both electronic and paperback form.

Since the original publication, J.E. Duke has continued to write and publish a series of detective novels featuring Milo Starr & Jordan Sutton

Here are some of his publications

Million-Dollar Fraud - *(Coming Soon)*

Honorable Assassin - *A Sutton & Starr Mystery (Book 2)*

She Works With Killers - *A Sutton & Starr Mystery (Book 1)*

Family Lies: Generations of Deceit - *A Mystery*

Never Too Late for Love - *A Love Story*

All books available for download and/or in print at most online retailers.

Visit the author's website. **www.jeduke.com**